MW01487867

What Mennonite Girls
Are Good For

John Simmons Short Fiction Award

What Mennonite Girls
Are Good For

Jennifer Sears

University of Iowa Press · Iowa City

University of Iowa Press, Iowa City 52242
Copyright © 2025 by Jennifer Sears
uipress.uiowa.edu
Printed in the United States of America

Cover design by TG Design
Interior design and typesetting by Sara T. Sauers
Printed on acid-free paper

This is a work of fiction. Names, characters, businesses, places, events, locales, and incidents are either products of the author's imagination or used in a fictitious manner. Any resemblance to actual persons, living or dead, or actual events is purely coincidental and not intended by the author.

Library of Congress Cataloging-in-Publication Data
Names: Sears, Jennifer, 1968– author
Title: What Mennonite Girls Are Good For / Jennifer Sears.
Description: Iowa City: University of Iowa Press, 2025. |
Identifiers: LCCN 2025013477 (print) | LCCN 2025013478 (ebook) |
    ISBN 9781685970499 paperback | ISBN 9781685970505 ebook
Subjects: LCGFT: Short stories
Classification: LCC PS3619.E2564 W43 2025 (print) |
    LCC PS3619.E2564 (ebook) | DDC 813/.6—dc23/eng/20250415
LC record available at https://lccn.loc.gov/2025013477
LC ebook record available at https://lccn.loc.gov/2025013478

In memory of my father, Earl Sears
And for Massimo, my mother, and my sisters

Forgive us our trespasses as we forgive, I softly

recite among strangers, remembering...

—JULIA SPICHER KASDORF, *Eve's Striptease*

Are you angels? he asks. Are you lost?

—MIRIAM TOEWS, *Women Talking*

Contents

What Mennonite Girls
Are Good For

Blessed Are the Children Who Know Not to Tell

Asunción

THEY ARE *blessed*, the fourth graders are told every day, and they believe it. *Blessed*, they fly out of their white school building toward the grass soccer field. *Blessed*, they crouch at the centerline and stare at each other. They kick the ball hard, run fast, and fall to the ground in piles, any excuse to burn off the shy curiosity growing in their hearts—blessed boys against the blessed girls beneath the blessed Paraguayan sun.

They are missionary children, familiar with God, who lives—they are told—in their hearts, in their lungs, in their prayers, in their songs, and in the devotions led twice a day by their beautiful teacher, a devout Christian and birder whose soft Georgia accent makes them feel how even Daniel in the Lion's Den is truly a love story.

Their teacher stumps them with strange questions about their Noah.

Was it a rock dove, a carrier pigeon, or a lonely lovebird he set loose in search of that olive branch, that promise of God's love? Details, children! He created each one.

When the Spanish teacher puts them in pairs to practice rolling their Rs—*¡Erre con erre guitarra!*—the children laugh. They could stare forever at each other's tongues!

During mango season, overripe fruits from an enormous tree plop loudly onto the clay roof of their classroom. At recess, the children rush outside and stare up at the branches. *See, Ruthie, how it offers itself to Heaven!*

They pick up the fruit that has fallen to the ground and tear off the tough skins, the bright orange pulp staining their fingers and tongues. The boys use pocketknives to cut open papayas, hollow out the black seeds, and offer slices to the girls who give them kisses, lightning quick, on the cheek in return.

Ruthie only takes papaya from Tomás, a Brazilian boy chauffeured from the Hill each morning in the back seat of a glittering gold car. Rachel, Ruthie's twin sister, favors Stevie, a loud-mouthed Southern Baptist who saw the Devil in person loading wood into the steam engine that chugged his family all the way to Montevideo.

Ruthie? Don't you believe? Parents never lie!

Kyoko loves Robert's long Anglican fingers. Josefina Orozco de Saba, who also lives on the Hill, refuses to eat things off trees like an *indio*—like some squatter's child.

Alice, refusing anything from anyone, insists she's fed on God's love alone and proves it with a swift kick to poor Maximilian's shins.

Like missionary children everywhere, these children have learned to love quickly and to expect sudden farewells.

"Quentin's left with his family for the bush, where they will translate the Book of John into three Guaraní dialects," their teacher tells them. "Let's pray for their safety. Let's pray for their courage."

"The Wongs' papers have come through—*Jesus watches those who persevere*—and they can finally leave for the States. Let's pray for their safe passage. Let's pray that they never feel alone."

Hush, children . . . pray for Teresa's mother, who has broken down again because she can't take this place anymore—Alfredo Stroessner, his pale face postered on every wall, the bullet holes in the streetlights, the sickness, the mosquitos, the children, always in need of more than anyone can give—those children who stand in front of the cathedral and hold out their hands, those children in the Plaza de la Democracia who wait by the counter at the lido bar to seize the empanada crusts from your finished plate. And she can't even think about the devil's heat that will curse them again come January.

Pray, children! their teacher says. Let us pray that He sends Teresa's mother comfort, that she feels again His enduring love.

Each morning, at the entrance of their school grounds, the children skip over the wooden grates that keep out the large yellow cows that sometimes wander onto the grassy boulevard in the middle of Avenida Santísimo Sacramento. Their small school compound holds a dozen whitewashed schoolrooms and buildings with red clay tiles, a handball court, a soccer field, and a small yellow chapel with a steeple. The Paraguayan groundsmen swish their long machetes through the air to trim the fruit trees that crowd the playgrounds. Their machetes swish around the bushes and just above the lawns and the soccer field. Always laughing and joking, the groundsmen keep the school grounds scrupulously clean except for the muddy creek that winds along the edge of the soccer field, and who could do anything about that?

Before the school day starts, the boys in the older grades play soccer with the Paraguayan men. The younger children scream from the sidelines as they watch the boys and men, all of those bodies move back and forth. They scream for no reason except to hear their own voices that make them feel alive in the beautiful world that surrounds them, the world that shows them so many *blessed* things.

When the chapel bell rings, the children race to form lines and file into their schoolrooms. The groundsmen, Doña Olga who makes empanadas for snacks, and everyone else on the grounds know to be silent. They know to listen as the children's songs spill through the windows, just as Ruthie knows to sit beside Alice.

Ruthie? Hear Alice sing! Now, don't you believe?
The morning prayers at the Christian academy have begun.

When the weather is warm, Ruthie, Rachel, and the other fourth-grade girls sneak off to the creek that borders the soccer field. They slip off their sandals and walk into the water. Rumors of bloodsuckers, hookworms, and underwater snakes both terrify and obsess them. Even their fears here are exotic! An excuse to pray loudly to God, *who is with them at all times.*

These girls know how to baptize each other! Hands held in prayer over her heart, each girl holds her body ramrod straight as the others pour water over her head. Water runs down her hair, over her eyes, and into her mouth as she gasps for air while the others shout blessings. A loving husband! Lots of babies! A life filled with songs!

The girls move into the ravine, each time a little farther than the last. On each side, the red clay banks rise higher as the water gets deeper, but the girls keep going. The water rises above their knees, weighing down and dirtying the hems of their dresses. Ruthie, in front, always wants to see around the bend. Alice holds tight behind her. Kyoko and Greta, the shy ambassadors' daughters, and beautiful Josefina Orozco de Saba keep up the center as sure-footed Rachel holds down the end.

Above them, the girls see Guaraní women laying clothes to dry on the rocks at the top of the ravine. They see Guaraní children, laughing and shouting. The missionary girls laugh back. The beauty of their surroundings always stuns them. They've seen flowers shaped and colored like strings of toucan bills, ferns and palms that shower the air with green, and trees with trunks shaped like enormous bottles burst into bloom for one day, their white petals covering the ground by nightfall. In this place, birds drop feathers in oranges, blues, and greens that people at home—*wherever that is*—would never believe.

To this beautiful world, the girls offer their songs. *¡Quiero cantar una linda canción!* they sing to the river. *I want to sing you a beautiful song* … they sing to birds. Their teacher tells them again and again that they are *her* creatures, that they are His creatures. Like parakeets, parrots, and macaws! They were sent to Paraguay to be messengers of His love.

Moving farther down the creek, the girls sing as loud as they can just to hear their voices returned in layers of sounds that delight and scare them. Is that only an echo . . . the land itself returning their songs? Or are birds or bats or other children teasing them from the top of the banks?

"A snake!" Alice always screams first. "Hurry back! Bloodsuckers everywhere!"

"Snake!" the girls all scream, even though everyone says Alice is a *liar-liar-liar!*

As the other girls pull her back, Ruthie looks down the river. She wants to go beyond the places they've seen together. She wants to laugh away a sadness growing inside her, a feeling that as much as her parents believe in *His* love—as much as everything she sees, she sees through *their* love—promises aren't always the truth.

Ruthie! Stay with us! Ruthie, come back!

Safe on the riverbank, the girls pick enormous green leaves to wipe off their legs and lie down on the rocks to let their clothes dry against their bodies. Kyoko frets over her dirty dress. The other girls wonder out loud where the boys are and practice what they are sure are provocative poses as Alice and Ruthie practice adult kisses. They sing their own Songs of Songs!

The girls all laugh except Rachel, who looks away and begins their father's favorite guitar song about doves and tears and other sad things that get caught in the wind.

Hippie, Alice calls Ruthie and Rachel's Mennonite father because he doesn't like churches with flags and because he wears jeans and T-shirts instead of creased pants and ironed shirts sealed off at the neck with a tie, like fathers are supposed to wear.

The girls settle down to rest. They love the feel of smooth rock warmed by the sun. They love the machete songs, the soccer songs, and the laughter of the Guaraní children. They love the bird songs, the river songs, the blowin'-in-the-wind songs, the prayer songs. They love the love songs that fill the whole country, which they know will never be their own.

Ruthie and Rachel live in a whitewashed cottage on a cobblestone street off Avenida Santísimo Sacramento. The houses and lots on their block huddle against the high wall that surrounds the grounds of a pink brick mansion. Like serfs—their father laughs as he tries to trim their lawn with a machete like the hired men who trim their school lawns. Their mother has gotten used to the washer, the hand-turned wringer, and the tiny clay-tiled kitchen, where she's learned to make arroz con pollo and sopa paraguaya to accompany recipes from her tattered *More-with-Less Cookbook*, brought from the States.

Daktari! On Tuesday and Thursday evenings, Ruthie and Rachel run next door to their landlady's house and wait with the other neighborhood children on the brick patio. Sweating and making a show of her effort, Doña Ysmarelda hauls out a small black-and-white television. Her two daughters follow, dragging an enormous folding chair they set directly in front of the screen. Doña Ysmarelda fiddles with the antenna until the volume crackles and the picture comes on. She lowers her body with an "Ay!" into the chair with one daughter stationed on each side, unless she chooses Ruthie or Rachel to sit there so she can run her fingers through their strange blonde hair.

Craning their necks to see around Doña Ysmarelda's massive pompadour, the neighborhood children crowd closer toward the screen—everyone except for the Guaraní boy whose family lives in the burned-down house across the street. He watches from the sidewalk because he doesn't even own a pair of beggars' thongs.

¡Pique!—hookworms! Doña Ysmarelda says whenever she shoos him back, saying she doesn't want his feet to infect her grounds. Ruthie closes her eyes. She wants to know why the Guaraní boy is so quiet, why he won't even tell them his name.

The children all love *Daktari*! They love the make-believe African jungle scenes that flash white-and-gray light across their faces and make them forget about the wild greens and deep reds that surround them.

They laugh at the jokes, even Ruthie and Rachel and the Guaraní boy who can't understand the Spanish words dubbed over the English. Though their mother has warned them not to show off, Ruthie and Rachel shout the English names as the credits roll down the screen at the end. *MGM . . . Clarence the Cross-Eyed Lion!*

Some nights after the show ends, Doña Ysmarelda dismisses the other children and calls Ruthie and Rachel and her daughters into the living room for dancing lessons. Sometimes they try balancing bottles on their heads like folkloric dancers they've seen downtown, but most nights she puts them in pairs and starts a record with weeping violins and a man who sings sad songs.

When the girls stop giggling and tripping over each other, Doña Ysmarelda sits on her couch and closes her eyes. Circling, circling, the girls keep dancing, pretending not to notice how Doña Ysmarelda wipes her eyes beneath her rhinestone glasses or how the long chains of glass tears that hang from the chandelier always tremble above them.

Everyone in the neighborhood knows the story. They all know who the father is. They've seen him arrive in his fancy white car every Wednesday at sundown and park in front of the house, engine idling as his daughters run outside to kiss his cheeks through the window as he hands them a white envelope filled with money.

Left them for a blonde German lady on the Hill. But who knows what's really true?

Ruthie wants to know if he ever looks back after his car pulls away, if he ever sees how Doña Ysmarelda steps out of the house and clutches the girls to her side as they watch his car sway down the cobblestone street and disappear into the stream of traffic on Avenida Santísimo Sacramento.

¿Por qué me enseñaron a amar si es volcar sin sentido los sueños al mar?

As the girls dance in front of Doña Ysmarelda's tears, Ruthie hears words she knows from Spanish class—love, dreams, the sea. She wants to know why the sadness inside that music sounds so unlike the songs they sing, why sadness feels more true.

Circling beneath the chandelier, the girls hold each other as Doña

Ysmarelda picks up the needle and makes the man on the record begin his tango again.

Sometimes Ruthie walks alone down Avenida Santísimo Sacramento to Alice's house and makes three short claps outside of the gate—*clap! clap! clap!*—the Paraguayan doorbell. Alice opens the door and brings her inside the high walls, where mango, avocado, and palm trees shade their bungalow and the wide porch, where a heart-shaped reed fan, a jug of real peacock feathers, and an American flag dutifully remind them of home-sweet-home Louisiana.

In late afternoons, Ruthie and Alice play in the trees while Pastor Arthur sits on the porch writing sermon notes he'll deliver in Guaraní at his church in the campo or thank-you letters to mission sponsors back home. His cheeks flush above his white collars knotted shut with a dark tie, no matter the heat. If the girls stay quiet, he offers them sips of iced tea made from leaves shipped from a believer in Louisiana or lets them sit next to him and roll bandages cut from sheets donated for the leprosy colony outside of Asunción.

But Alice and Ruthie rarely win such honor. As they climb the trees, their voices rise higher until Pastor Arthur calls out, "Alice!"

"Sir!" Alice never calls him Daddy. "We'll settle down now, sir!" she says.

What Ruthie loves best at Alice's house is the parrot cage beside the kitchen door. The girls crawl across the yard and leap in front of the bird who cocks his iridescent head and shrieks, *I am an eagle!*—words learned from an only son, gone forever from this Paraguayan home.

"Liar," seventeen-year-old Dinah hisses when Mama makes her feed the parrot slices of papaya.

Taking care not to smudge her painted fingernails, Dinah shuts the metal door and tells them the parrot's jungle squawks, sharp beak, and nervous pink tongue are signs of the Devil.

I am an eagle—the bird cries with its strange voice.

"We all know where liars go," she says.

After Dinah leaves, Alice and Ruthie run to the cage. "I am a parrot, a parrot," they say over and over, trying to save him from Hell, to teach him the Truth.

Prayers and devotions fill Alice's white bungalow before and after each meal, at midafternoon, and once again at bedtime. During Bible recitations around the dining table, Pastor Arthur goes first, followed by Mama and Dinah, who closes her sparkling blue eyelids. A true Southern belle, Ruthie's mother has explained, and a lonely one at that.

Ruthie's family hardly ever does recitations. At Alice's table, she sometimes confuses Bible verses with lines from Bible songs. "Let the little children come to me."

"Matthew 19:14," Alice adds.

"Half a verse," Dinah says.

"Jesus wept," Ruthie says. "John 11:35."

"Cheat," Dinah says.

Silly Ruthie. The shortest verse in the Bible. Everyone knows that!

Alice loves the Psalms more than anything. She sets verses to her own tunes as Pastor Arthur whacks the table with his palm. "That's it, child," he always says.

Ruthie has seen Pastor Arthur pull off his belt and make Alice kneel on the ground. She's seen long red welts rise across her back as she confesses how she *disobeys-disobeys-disobeys.* But when Alice sings her Psalms, Pastor Arthur's eyes burn hard and tight with love.

"Your gift, child," he says.

When Alice receives compliments, she never blushes or looks away like little girls are supposed to do. "Thank you, sir," she only says.

David . . . David! Some nights, when the family goes silent with prayer, the parrot outside the kitchen door cries out—*David! David!*— until Mama can't take it anymore and runs for the biggest kitchen knife. Still, the family bows. Still, the family prays as Mama runs out the back door to strike the long metal blade against the cage.

David! David! the bird cries. The name of her only son who died in a different jungle.

Vietnam, Ruthie's mother has whispered—*don't ever say it*—his body never found.

As the family sits at the table, heads bowed, listening to Mama's blade strike the cage, Ruthie wants to know what happens to those little girls who, like the parrot, repeat the wrong words. What happens to children who tell stories of things they shouldn't have seen?

David! David! the bird cries.

It's Mama voice the bird has memorized like so many recitations of love, her words calling her son home for prayers at night.

In early December just before summer heat sets in, Ruthie and Rachel and the other fourth graders crowd into the school van for a program at the leprosy colony. As they leave the cluttered streets of Asunción, they sing "With Christ in Your Boat You Can Smile at the Storm" and then in Spanish, "Con Cristo in tu barco. . . ." As sugarcane fields open on both sides of the highway, they practice "Jesus Loves Me" in Guaraní, Spanish, and Swahili because their teacher served in Tanzania before the Lord decided she belonged in Paraguay.

When they turn off the highway, the road narrows. Jungle leaves filter the sunlight around them. Branches brush against the roof of the van. When the roads get even smaller, grass rushes below them. They are surrounded by green!

The van stops on the edge of the quarantined compound, and the children step into a hushed otherworld. Their teacher clutches her binoculars. *Tit-tit-tut!* she shouts, her favorite call. "Just a glimpse!" she says and runs off, abandoning them.

Silenced, the children hold on to each other.

Their parents have told them to beware of wild dogs and poisonous snakes. They've been told to watch out for scorpions and tarantulas that cover the ground at night, for frogs that creep up through the sewers and glow in the dark. But sometimes Ruthie feels there must be something more that makes the adults so afraid. As if, despite the beauty of His world, there were places from which children never return, places like Vietnam or leprosy colonies, places where even God fails—

Silly, Ruthie! God never fails!

—where even His love can't save you.

The teacher returns, face flushed. "Children!" she says, as if she's only just remembered them.

They've read about lepers, the blind, and the lame all their lives— *Jesus touched them! He healed them!*—but as they walk toward the cluster of buildings, the children are a little nervous. "Mama told me not to touch a leper," Josefina whispers. "Not even if one needs a hug."

The children are lined up in the dining hall, where the residents sit in rows. Their teacher has told them no one visits them except doctors and nurses and missionary workers, that some of their families believe they are cursed, but Ruthie isn't sure anymore what is and isn't true.

Jesus wept. *Silly, Ruthie! Why did he weep?*

¡Quiero cantar una linda canción! The children sing the songs they practiced in the van, the songs they sing in their classrooms, on the playground, in chapel, in church, and at home. They sing songs they've sung so many times Ruthie hardly hears the words inside them.

As they sing, a man raises his arms. A woman claps her fingerless hands. A young boy standing in the back of the room opens and closes his mouth as if imitating them. His skin is the color of the wooden walls and the trunks of the trees that surround them. As she sings, Ruthie wants to know if he's been quarantined there his whole life. She wants to know if, after absorbing so much green air and soaking his body in the same rain, he's grown roots into the ground around them.

¡Quiero cantar una linda canción! . . . I want to sing you a beautiful song, the missionary children sing, offering their message, their promise of His love.

Ruthie closes her eyes. Something. Not right. How can she be the messenger, when she doesn't know the message?

Silly, Ruthie! Don't you believe?

On and on, they sing the songs missionary children sing everywhere. *Blessed* are the children who sing so many prayers! *Blessed* are the girls and boys who sing for the sick and the poor. *Blessed* are the children who sing promises of His love and then fly away from jungles and hospitals and schoolrooms, away from neighborhoods and soccer fields and sorrows and tangos.

Something. Not right. Ruthie keeps her eyes shut as she sings.

Singing and praying, praying and singing. *Blessed* are the children who are told when they sing—*they-are-good, they-are-good, they-are-good*.

Some nights, Ruthie and Rachel and the neighborhood children play hide-and-seek. They squeeze between hedges and flower beds in Doña Ysmarelda's garden. They crouch inside the empty monkey cage. They hide in the trees and grasses surrounding the burned-down house where the Guaraní boy lives. They sneak up on Ruthie and Rachel's mother as she practices her Paraguayan harp beneath the porch light.

"Children?" Her fingers stiffen over the strings. "Children!" she sighs when she hears their laughter.

The children run in front of the gate of the pink mansion behind their houses until the security guard shoos them away with a shout. Laughing still, they fly down the street, trying not to stumble over the cobblestones in the dark.

The Guaraní boy runs easily over the stones in his bare feet. When he hides, no one can hardly ever find him, but one night, Ruthie finds him lying in a ditch beneath a bush. *¡Indio! ¡Indio!* the other neighborhood children shout as Ruthie crawls next to him. He doesn't move. She kisses his arm. He doesn't move. She tries to kiss him again, this time like Alice sometimes kisses her. She tastes salt and sweat and chicle.

The boy cries out, and then he's running *away-away-away* from her—over the cobblestones and under the barbed wire that surrounds his house.

Ruthie! The other children call out.

Something, *not right*. She didn't mean to scare him.

Despite the Song of Songs, despite love stories in the Bible, everything they've learned about their bodies is either dark or an embarrassment. Missionary children know without being told that their bodies are things to fly away from. Beneath the moon's blank white eye, she presses her body into the ground. A vine imprints its vegetable soul into her thigh. Dirt cakes beneath her fingernails. She is no longer certain which kingdom she belongs to, earth or sky.

Ruthie!

She is no longer hiding. She is waiting for the message to find her, waiting for her message to deliver, some promise of God's love. But what if her message never comes?

When the other children have all gone home, Ruthie runs back to their bungalow, passing her mother, who still plays her harp beneath the porch light.

"Where did you go, Ruthie?" Rachel asks when she enters.

"I don't know." Remembering how the boy cried out and the feel of the vine that pressed against her thigh, she hides her face in her pillow.

The girls lie in the dark listening to their mother begin again her best song, the first piece the Paraguayan maestro, Señor Fernando Cáceres, teaches all the embassy and missionary women who come to him for lessons. *Despedida.* Farewell.

On nights when Ruthie stays over at Alice's house, they share her single bed, their bodies burning against each other. A screen window opens to the porch but no matter how hot the nights get, Alice wants the window *shut-shut-shut.*

Don't you know, Ruthie? Snakes can always get in!

Ruthie asks Alice if she thinks there will be butcher knives in Heaven, like the one Mama uses to make the parrot stop? Ruthie asks Alice what happens to little girls who sing the wrong words, who tell stories of things they shouldn't have seen?

Silly Ruthie, don't you know? Everything is in God's hands!

In whispers, Alice tells Ruthie stories about people she left behind in Louisiana. Aunt Lil' lost an arm, but she still plays the accordion good, *cross-my-heart-hope-to-die.* Her neighbor, a famous scientist, blew up his own hand, but now he has a wooden one covered with a kidskin glove. He lets her hold it sometimes. And if you listen to the Louisiana wind close enough, you can hear it whispering scripture, offering songs of His love, and when the moon comes out, werewolves wait for you in the trees. *Follow me, child*, that's what werewolves sing.

Liar—liar—liar, Rachel calls Alice. But Ruthie isn't so certain.

In the dark, Alice's stories go on. How Dinah sometimes touches herself there, for real. She's seen her through the bedroom window. And how Pastor Arthur isn't her real daddy. He's her uncle, swear to God! And Mama's not her real mama, she just calls her that. Her real daddy did such mysterious things to her in the night. Alice likes to show Ruthie things her real daddy did, wet things, tickly things—*what funny noises their little girl bodies can make!*—and things that hurt, just a little.

Alice says she even saw her real daddy cry.

Silly Alice, real daddies don't cry!

Papers are coming from Louisiana, Alice says, papers that will make Pastor Arthur and Mama and Dinah her real family. "They want to make me their own," she says.

Ruthie squeezes her eyes shut whenever Alice talks about the papers. Sometimes when they walk home from school, Alice runs down Avenida Santísimo Sacramento calling out, "The papers are here! Today! I can feel it!" In the beginning, Ruthie believed her. She wanted to come too and see the papers arrive in what she believed had to be ceremonious boxes. She imagined Pastor Arthur unraveling great scrolls that would make Alice his very own girl.

But the papers never come.

Alice cries, sometimes, about the papers. She doesn't ever want to go back to her real daddy in Louisiana. She wants to stay with Pastor Arthur and Mama and Dinah. Pastor Arthur has promised her that by singing she'll make herself clean. Alice says she'll sing her Psalms for anyone. She'll sing in Spanish. She'll sing in Guaraní. She'll sing whatever Pastor Arthur or their teacher want her to sing. She'll be very good. She only wants to stay in Paraguay forever.

All night, Ruthie and Alice sleep with their arms around each other—*Silly Alice! I already told you I love you!* As Alice pulls Ruthie's hands to her body and puts her hands *everywhere-everywhere-everywhere*—they hear insects smack their wings against the window-panes and creatures scurry across the front porch. But these girls are no longer afraid of such sounds. It's the peacock feathers that make them nervous, staring in when the moon is bright.

Through a crack in the wall behind Doña Ysmarelda's house, the neighborhood children spy on the pink mansion with its wide lawn and collie dogs. They watch cars with dark windows circle the drive and chauffeurs open doors for people who emerge wearing fancy clothes. They've seen Cecilia, the rich girl who never smiles.

When the servant from the pink mansion comes to Ruthie and Rachel's house and tells their mother that Cecilia wants to meet them, the whole neighborhood sees. The neighborhood children follow Ruthie and Rachel and the servant down the cobblestone street. *¡Rubias! ¡Rubias!* the children shout, even after the security guard locks the gate behind them. Ruthie and Rachel follow the servant up the long drive to the front door, where a maid wearing a white apron rushes them through hallways with high ceilings and chandeliers to a sunroom with enormous windows that overlook a swimming pool.

"Misioneras," Cecilia says when Ruthie and Rachel enter.

Cecila sits on a couch. Around her are other skinny girls with long shiny hair and older-girl makeup. Two smoke cigarettes. A sad girl stares out the window. The American song that's playing everywhere in Asunción, on street corners where boys sell newspapers and on the jukebox in the bowling alley, plays from a cassette player, "50 Ways to Leave Your Lover."

Cecilia throws a white pillow on the floor in the center of the room and tells Ruthie and Rachel to sit.

As she crosses the thick white carpet, Ruthie feels like she's floating in front of the beautiful girls in the beautiful house. She and Rachel are birds! Together, they float down to the pillow. From the floor, Ruthie sees the wooden table in front of them has legs carved like mermaids with bare round breasts and tails that reach up and split open to hold the tabletop.

Cecilia gives Ruthie and Rachel a pencil and paper and puts the cassette player in front of them. She starts the song from the beginning. As the drums begin like heartbeat, Cecilia tells them to write down the words.

"For our English class," another girl explains before she coughs over a cigarette.

"Save us, misioneras," Cecilia says, and starts laughing.

Ruthie and Rachel do as they are told. Starting and stopping the cassette player, they write down the words—*lover, leave, free!* They don't stop when the maid sets a plate of cakes in front of them. They don't stop when the girl with bloodshot eyes runs her fingers through their hair the way Doña Ysmarelda does sometimes—they've gotten used to that in Paraguay.

Floating, floating on sunlight held up by mermaids with naked breasts, Ruthie and Rachel keep writing. The "50 Ways" fold into verses. The words fold into a psalm, even though the singer's voice trails off sometimes, as if he only half believes what he sings, only half wants to get himself free.

Ruthie and Rachel finish and hold up the paper. Sunlight shines through it. Lit by *His* love—*lover, leave, free!*—their letters as light as air! But the beautiful girls don't notice this. The girl with glistening eyes holds a pair of scissors. "May I?" she asks.

Blessed are the children, so meek and so mild, who do as they are told. *Blessed* are the children who hold perfectly still, even when everything moves slowly and silently, they hear the blade slice through their hair. *Blessed* are the children who've been taught to trust Him, who've been taught to-be-kind. *Blessed* are the children who obey.

Laughing, the girl mixes the two locks, blonde into blonde. She stands in the middle of the room and puts the hair between her legs— over her private parts—and starts a naughty dance. *Rubia!* she laughs as the hair sways.

"Dance with me," she says to Ruthie and Rachel as the man on the cassette tape finally begins a new song.

Doing as they are told, Ruthie and Rachel dance for the rich girls. They dance together like Doña Ysmarelda has taught them—like *los pobres* one girl laughs. Rachel stops, but Ruthie keeps dancing. She wants to dance forever in that white light. She'll dance for rich girls and mermaids. She'll dance for Doña Ysmarelda and her tears. She doesn't understand why so many lovers want to leave or why table legs sometimes have such beautiful breasts.

"Stop!" the sad girl by the window says, but Ruthie keeps her eyes closed. Like Alice, she only knows she wants to stay in Paraguay forever. She'll be good, she'll be very good.

Ruthie's still dancing when everything ends at once. The music gets turned off. The maid takes their hands.

"Gracias, misioneras!" Cecilia says as the other girls laugh.

As they're pulled away, Ruthie turns back and sees that the room filled with bright light has turned entirely white, the cakes melting beneath their white frosting, the bored older girls holding white cigarettes, their blonde hair draping across a white dish that sits on a silver tray.

"I didn't like it," Rachel whispers as the old servant rushes them through the front door and down the long drive. The servant walks as if he wants to get them *far-far* away from the older girls.

After being in that mansion with its wide staircases, enormous windows, and so much light, the other houses in their neighborhood look dirtier, the cobblestone streets too narrow. Their whitewashed bungalow, where everyone waits for them on the veranda, looks like a hut.

"Very good little girls," the servant from the mansion tells their mother as he hands her a box filled with cakes.

After he leaves, everyone wants to know what they saw in the pink mansion. Ruthie and Rachel describe the maid and her fancy uniform, the white pillows and carpets, the room filled with light, and the skinny rich girls who wouldn't touch the cakes.

"Ay!" Doña Ysmarelda's oldest girl sighs as she reaches into the open box. "Ay!" she says again, and even though she is smiling, Ruthie hears how she sounds like Doña Ysmarelda lying on the couch, listening to sad music, sighing about love.

Lover, leave, free! Ruthie tells them how they wrote down the words to that song about the "50 Ways" and how they danced for the rich girls in the middle of the room. She tells them the pool was filled with white lilies. There was the scent of flowers everywhere. Ruthie tells them how very nice those girls were to them.

"Sing for us!" the others say. "Sing the song."

Liar, liar, liar! Rachel stares at Ruthie as she begins the song.

Everyone laughs. Everyone sings! Everyone knows the "50 Ways to Leave..."

Ruthie closes her eyes and starts dancing. *Lover, leave, free!*

Blessed are the children who know not to tell how they looked back, who remember Lot's wife, who know it's easier for a camel to squeeze itself through the eye of a needle than for beautiful rich girls to get into Heaven. *Blessed* are the children who know not to tell how soft and beautiful that other world was, how she loves that man's voice, who *know-know-know* not to tell how they saw the mermaids' round breasts or how that silly girl held their hair between her legs or how strange their blonde hair looked draping off the dish and onto the silver tray.

Wearing their best dresses, Ruthie and Rachel and their mother take a bus to the Hill. As they walk down a wide avenue counting jacaranda trees, their mother tells them they must start a list. She reminds them she too had been a missionary girl, she too fell in love with a place called Aibonito, where poinsettias grew as big as trees. She too had to leave. A list, she says, of things they want to remember. Like jacaranda trees with lavender flowers. That man they saw walking a white horse into Lago Ypacaraí as the sunset turned the water and sky bright orange around them. The midnight soccer game with the ball made of fire. The day hundreds of believers crawled up the mountain to Caacupé to kiss the tiny Virgin of Miracles.

"But what about Alice?" Ruthie asks.

Alice, who can't go home to Louisiana. She'll never leave Alice or put her on a list. And what about David, who can't come home from Vietnam? Or the boy in the leper colony who has to stay in one place, maybe forever.

A guard lets them through a security gate in front of an ambassador's white house, where the students of Señor Fernando Cáceres have gathered to celebrate the maestro's new recording. Ruthie and Rachel, the only children, are given cakes and led into a courtyard with green-tinted windows and birdcages that rise to the ceiling.

Inside their cages, the birds flutter their wings and stare at the fake jungle leaves painted on the walls around them, as if they too were remembering. Moving from cage to cage, Ruthie tries to imagine her life without macaws and toucans, without the other birds their teacher has taught them to see, without the parrot behind Alice's house who believes he's an eagle.

Liar, liar, liar.

A sweeping glissando sounds from the concert room. The maestro starts tuning his strings. The birds grow restless. On her list, there won't be any cages.

Ruthie and Rachel go into the concert room. Señor Cáceres sits in the front. He wears the plain green shirt he always wears. As he listens, his eyes look, as always, as if he's been crying.

Ruthie sees all at once things she isn't supposed to see. Her mother, smiling too hard as she shifts from foot to foot in her flat shoes in front of the rich ladies with their slender ankles and high heels. The sweat staining and dampening the maestro's green shirt.

Señor Cáceres plucks an open string with a long fingernail. He touches his heart. As the women keep talking, he pulls the instrument to his chest and begins.

¡Aquí! Ruthie has seen Señor Cáceres press his fist into his heart, trying to teach her mother how she must listen. *¡Aquí!* Señor Cáceres's fingers free his song from his strings. *¡Aquí!*—in his music without words, in music with so many sorrows mixed in.

The women take their seats.

Ruthie wonders if Señor Cáceres is tired of the ladies, tired of playing songs that sound like the birds and trains, songs for bottle trees in bloom. But as he bows his head, she hears.

¡Aquí! Here, here must be love.

Alice! Where is Alice?

Sent back to Louisiana. Their teacher explains the sudden absence of one more friend. How the Lord has a different plan for her than this Paraguayan home.

The children stay silent as their teacher praises Alice's family, the mighty strength of their faith, how God's voice will always move through Alice with His gift of song. The children are told what they are always told. To be grateful for each day they have together. To trust in His will. To remember they are *blessed*!

Rachel slides Ruthie an eraser shaped like an elephant because she knows Ruthie likes it.

Pray, children! their teacher says. Pray that we all meet again in Paradise!" She reminds them how they too will fly away. Like birds, they'll sing their songs into the sky.

Silly Ruthie. No one stays in Paraguay forever!

Despedida. Farewell.

When the children run to the soccer field at recess, Ruthie runs from one friend to the other—Kyoko, Greta, Rachel, Josefina, Stevie, Maximilian, and Tomás—laughing about nothing, being a ridiculous girl.

A bird flies low and calls to them. "Tit-tit-tut!" the children shout back as the bird circles higher above them.

"Alice!" Ruthie shouts.

Everywhere she sees Alice. Alice standing by the creek, waiting for her. Alice hanging from the trees, her back lined with welts from Pastor Arthur's belt. Alice, whose voice sounds like no one else's. Alice, who can't ever sing beautifully enough, no matter how hard she tries. Alice, whose real daddy—

The bird calls out again.

"Alice!" Ruthie shouts. *Alice-Alice-Alice!*

When the teacher comes to call them inside, the children rush toward her. "It's Alice! The bird is speaking to us! *Cross-our-hearts-and-hope...*"

"What did she say?"

"Tit-tit-tut!" Stevie laughs. "Tit-tit-tut!" the other children shout.

But Ruthie opens her arms wide and begins to whirl. "I am an eagle!" she shouts. *Liar, liar, liar.*

"I am an eagle," the other children shout.

"I am an eagle!" Ruthie shouts as she turns and turns until she falls to the ground, staring up at the sky, which they've all been told—

Silly Ruthie . . . don't you believe?

—is Heaven.

Sins and Symbols

Sins and Symbols

NOW THAT SHE WAS skinny, Ruthie loved to take off her clothes for him. She just wished he would look at her. She sat on a folding chair centered on a white canvas tarp. A spotlight was directed on her.

"How long?" she asked.

One board of set lights brightened the tarp. Ruthie sat straighter. She smiled, but he switched off the lights again.

"You're never ready," Ruthie said.

Nathan didn't respond.

When Ruthie whined, Nathan always said she sounded even younger than thirteen.

It was summer outside in Southern California, but the warm light was blocked from the room. Bricks filled the tall windowpanes where stained glass had once been. Wind circled inside the sealed-off steeple above them. She could hear his sandals scuff against the cement floor. The metal chair was cold against her skin.

Both boards of set lights came on.

"The usual," Nathan called out, as if they ever started with something new.

Ruthie smiled. She tossed her hair and stretched her arms and began what he called their "warm-ups." Nathan crouched beside the tarp, watching her through the viewfinder. She knew he hadn't loaded any film. He was an old man, he'd explained the first day she came to the studio. He needed to play certain games to get into the mood.

Ruthie stared into the camera's enormous telescoping lens.

"Play," he said.

Ruthie lifted her hips off the chair, remembering a picture from a magazine he had her study. "Like a Virgin," the article was titled, riffing on the pop song playing everywhere that summer. In the pictures, a tiny acrobat stretched her legs in the splits, eyes closed, back arched, hair falling down her spine. *Suzalie would love to be an Olympic gymnast,* the caption read, *if daddy would only let her out of the house!*

To Ruthie, Suzalie looked so beautiful, so strange. She knelt on the tarp. Her hip joints popped as she tried to force her legs into Suzalie's impossible position.

"Jesus Christ," Nathan said. "What's that?"

Ruthie released her limbs. She could never do anything right.

"I'm stretching," she said. "Can't I stretch?" She slid into poses they'd practiced, ones he'd approved. Remembering she just put on lipstick, Ruthie did the look-like-you're-blowing-a-bubble thing with her mouth. She grabbed her hair and tousled it on top of her head.

"Good girl," Nathan whispered. "Good girl. That's it." Finally, he pulled a film case from his pocket and loaded it into the camera.

Ruthie held her pose. *Perfectly perfect,* she wanted him to say. At 103 pounds, she even felt smaller beneath the cathedral ceilings and set lights. Nathan never mentioned her weight loss. It had come off surprisingly fast. A sign, she believed, though she wasn't certain of what.

"Look at me," Nathan said, lifting the camera to his eye.

Yes . . . the film whispered as it advanced between pictures. *Yes*, she heard when she listened a certain way.

"I am looking," she said.

Yes . . . yes . . . yes. "Good girl."

Good girl. Perfectly perfect. Ruthie stared back at him. Enormous glasses with thick lenses magnified his small eyes. Colorless old lips. Odd fingers—thin with round, bulging tips—frog fingers. She moved her eyes down his chest. Damp with sweat, his white shirt already clung to his skin. Nothing about Nathan ever changed.

Yes . . . yes . . . yes.

"Why is there always wind in that steeple?" she asked. "Even when it's not a windy day, I hear wind."

"Why always why?" Nathan said, making his voice childlike, mocking her.

"I'm not a kid," Ruthie said.

"You're still a kid."

Ruthie turned abruptly toward the back of the sanctuary and walked away from him. Everyone wanted her to stay a stupid kid. "Let the little children come to me. . . ." Matthew 19. Verse 14. She heard her own voice reciting the words.

"Not so far," Nathan called.

Ruthie stepped onto a raised platform behind the tarp where Nathan stored larger set pieces from the theater productions he directed during the school year. The Chancel, he called it. Gashes in the floorboards marked where a pulpit once stood.

Ruthie looked back.

Nathan had attached his bulky flash to the top of his camera, slid off his sandals, and stepped onto the white tarp.

Ruthie turned her butt to face him.

"That's it," she heard him say.

She spread her legs.

"Hold that." *Yes . . . yes . . . yes*, the film said.

She'd learned things since she'd met him. To talk less as they "worked," that was one thing. To move more slowly. She'd learned that too. As she looked over her shoulder, she remembered to avoid squinting into the flash. She wanted to remember everything.

Beside the tarp, Nathan's "Collection"—tiny bikinis, a ruffled little-girl gown, a gauzy robe with a feathered hem, a lacy teddy, everything white, everything sized extra small—trembled on a portable ballet barre. In contrast to the stone walls and wooden pews, everything about their afternoons—the tarp, the fold-up lights and metal chair, the portable barre—was temporary, designed to disappear.

Yes . . . yes . . . yes . . .

After tomorrow, she'd disappear too. It was her last day in California, though Nathan didn't know it. Her family had the car almost packed. They would leave the next morning.

The boards creaked as Nathan stepped onto the platform behind her.

Ruthie moved toward a backdrop from the previous semester's production. "A dreary Russian classic," he'd called it. She leaned her cheek into the backdrop, just to be funny. Dried moss scratched her skin. "I liked how those pictures came out with the tundra. Remember? 'Little Girl in the Tundra.'"

Nathan's breath fell on her shoulder.

He stood so close to her, she started. He laughed.

She was most beautiful when she got nervous, he often said. That was why he needed to scare her sometimes.

She opened her mouth the way he liked.

"That's it. Now, relax." Relax, he always said, though his fingers shook so much at times he could hardly press the button down.

The light flashed again, whitening her skin.

Yes . . . yes . . . yes. She shivered, hoping he wouldn't see.

"Now, look at yourself," he whispered.

She looked down. Green flakes from the set stained her chest and stomach.

He laughed. "There's a clean towel in the bathroom."

Ruthie rushed off the stage. Bits of dried moss fell onto the tarp as she ran toward his Collection and searched for the shawl made of thin white silk. She wrapped it around her shoulders. Long fringed tassels brushed the backs of her knees.

"We're leaving tomorrow," Ruthie called out. "We're going home."

She hadn't intended to tell him. She'd wanted to disappear, to think of him the following Wednesday waiting for her beside the empty lit-up tarp. But, for no reason at all, she'd gone and ruined everything.

Inside the bathroom, Ruthie locked the door and flicked a switch that activated a garland of Christmas lights circling a mirror above the sink. The red lights flashed on and off as she rinsed the dead moss from her chest. She closed the toilet lid and sat down. As she looked up, she saw a forgotten crucifix hanging high above the sink in front of her. With each pulse of light, the emaciated holy body appeared and disappeared. A white loincloth circled his sharp hip bones. Beneath his exaggerated rib cage, she saw a shadowy, hollow softness.

Ruthie brought her knees to her chest, covering her body with the shawl.

The day before, she'd weighed herself at the gym. 103 pounds. Ruthie and her mother had been on the Scarsdale Diet all summer, eating pink California grapefruits by the dozen. Ruthie's father swore that if he ever had to stare into the eye of that halved fruit again, he'd . . . but he never finished his ultimatums. Some evenings, he even ran with Ruthie along a bicycle path huddled against the foothills of the San Bernardino Mountains.

The family had arrived in town the last week of May so her father could complete summer research at the theology school. Aside from his few colleagues and the campus gardener, a perpetual postdoc and specialist on the Shroud of Turin, Ruthie and her twin sister didn't know anyone there. They spent most evenings watching TV as their father and the gardener sat on the patio arguing about civil injustices or communal leadership theory, her father's field of study. But they always finished with a heated debate over the authenticity of the Shroud, their favorite quibble.

The screen window separating the patio and living room filtered their phrases. Her father's rational musings—it was the message that mattered, the actions and responsibilities the holy body was meant to inspire—inflamed the specialist's passionate conviction. The Shroud was imprinted with the true image of Christ, he'd insist. To believe what can't be believed . . . to believe what others saw as impossible—that was the purest devotion, the purest act of faith.

"Drunkard," their mother whispered. Some nights she even yanked the curtain shut, insisting she could smell liquor on him. "That man is a drunkard," she'd say, discouraging Ruthie and Rachel from being friendly to him.

Ruthie had never heard the word "drunkard." It sounded exotic, something she associated with the man's trembling fingers, his earthy smell, and the tears she'd seen one afternoon when he called her toward a flower bed and showed her the laminated image of the Shroud he carried in his chest pocket. Slanting the card away from the sun's glare, Ruthie stared at the ghostly face—gray shadows marking where His eyes might have been, hollowed cheekbones, the vague outline of the solemn mouth, His bony fingers splayed across His special parts.

"It's beautiful," she said.

"Beautiful," the gardener said. He pressed the image to his lips and held it there before he slid it into his pocket. "Beauty. Yes. That's what it is. But don't tell your father. He doesn't understand."

Then he bent forward and, with a grunt, ripped a handful of sagebrush from the sandy soil, exposing the torn roots, shocked and new to the sun.

A uniform prettiness numbed the college town. Palm trees divided the centers of wide boulevards. Enormous flowers spilled over walls. Sprinklers chirped over garishly green lawns, offering glimpses of phony rainbows. Without the distraction of their friends, Rachel practiced her violin for hours while Ruthie devoted mornings to exercise and early afternoons to developing a suntan on the flat, tarpaper roof of their student housing unit, slices of cucumber laid over her eyes to protect them from wrinkles.

In late afternoons, she walked to a neglected botanical garden she'd found by chance just after they'd arrived, preferring most an area marked: OUR NATIVE LANDS (No Picnics). There, a footpath ended beneath a scrappy tree shading a wooden bench with a brass placard screwed into the seatback that read—

In Memory of Mrs. Robert K. Mueller
Devoted Teacher
Adored by Loved Ones and Students
and forgotten

Ruthie had added the last line, pressing the letters into the dried wood with a ballpoint pen.

Ruthie spent hours on Mrs. Robert K. Mueller's bench copying calorie charts and fat-free recipes from library books. Other times, she practiced ballet steps or poked sticks at the stupid toads and lizards that crawled out to warm in the sun.

She met Nathan there in the middle of June. Wearing a wide-brimmed canvas hat, he waved at her from the gate. Ruthie waved back, to-be-kind. As he made his way toward her, she straightened her sundress over her legs, irritated he'd intruded on what she'd come to consider her private garden.

"I saw you watching that frog," Nathan said when he reached her. He made the predictable link—frogs, princes. She gave no response. Fiddling with the brim of his hat, he asked if he could sit beside her.

Ruthie shrugged.

The bench shook as he sat down, pestering her with foolish guessing games until she gave him what he wanted. Ruthie. "Just turned fourteen." Ruthie had been taught all her life to-be-kind. It was her duty to-be-kind even when she didn't feel like it.

"I've seen you here before," Nathan went on. "I see how much you love this garden. You look like a princess sitting here."

"Thank you," Ruthie said to-be-kind.

He told Ruthie he was a drama professor at a local college. And a photographer. "I'd love to take your picture," he said. "You'd make a wonderful model."

Ruthie looked up. She'd admired pictures in fashion magazines but had never dreamed of being in them. "For real?"

Nathan complimented her smile, though Ruthie didn't think she'd smiled. He pulled out a flyer for a local Shriners carnival and, on an empty corner, tried to sketch directions to his drama lab, but his hands shook so much he could hardly press the pen into the paper.

Ruthie felt sorry for him, flabby and pathetic beneath his enormous hat. "Let me help you," she said, reaching toward his hand, but Nathan recoiled as if she'd moved to strike him.

He laid the map beside her when he finished. "Tomorrow," he said. The same time would be "perfectly perfect." At the gate, he waved until Ruthie waved in return.

In the apartment, Ruthie hid the flyer in a library book. Her father commented on her silence at dinner, but the subject was forgotten as the family watched a documentary detailing the upcoming wedding of Prince Charles and Lady Diana Spencer. "Still a girl!" her mother remarked as the almost princess blushed and blinked and beautifully pushed away her blonde bangs that kept falling into her eyes.

Before Ruthie got into bed, she stared in the mirror for a long time.

The next afternoon, instead of going to the garden, Ruthie walked to the college near the public library, holding the map in her hand. Her path coincided with a woman walking precariously on stiletto heels, clutching the leash of a tiny Chihuahua. The flip-flop of Ruthie's thongs, the click of the woman's heels, and the anxious tap of the dog's claws on the pavement continued in rhythm all the way to the campus green.

When Ruthie crossed the street and left them, the dog yipped and snarled. "Let her go," Ruthie heard the woman say. "Let the little girl go."

On the green, clusters of bushes, flowers, and blooming trees lined a central walk. One tree produced bouquets of pink and purple blossoms that fell whole to the ground, but when Ruthie pressed the petals to her nose, she found they had no scent. White mission-style buildings with Spanish archways were interspersed between dark brick buildings. A bagpiper practiced inside a courtyard, the airy drone starting and stopping in the hazy afternoon.

Ruthie couldn't imagine the green crowded with bodies and books. The summer campus seemed like an abandoned kingdom, just as her father's school did.

She found the old stone chapel with a yellow door—just as Nathan had written on the map. Seeing no one aside from the bagpiper absorbed in his playing, she opened the heavy door and stepped inside.

"Hello?"

No one answered.

The door closed behind her. Disoriented in the dark, Ruthie reached for a wall and touched cold, damp stone.

She heard footsteps in an adjacent room. After a second door opened, Ruthie realized she'd been standing inside a vestibule.

"You're here," Nathan said as he reached behind her to slide a bolt across the door. "You're really here."

Instead of answering, Ruthie entered the sanctuary. Ceilings arched upward, disappearing in shadows. Rows of deteriorating wooden pews were divided by a long center aisle. At the far end of the aisle, set lights illuminated a metal chair centered on a white tarp.

"You're so quiet," Nathan said.

Speaking in a rush, he launched into a history about his beloved drama lab, how the college had gone from a private to a public institution decades ago, how administrators kept threatening to sell the wooden pews and turn the building into a function hall, and how protesters who'd been allowed to spread sleeping bags across the stone floor during the "war years" had broken the stained-glass windows. Nathan's voice wavered as he described that old harm. "A violation is a violation," he said, even though the brick-and-mortar replacements created the darkness he needed for his work. For his rehearsals and theater productions. And for his "special" projects. Like this one.

He turned. Then, he laughed.

Ruthie had already walked onto the tarp.

"You're waiting," he said. "Perfect. We'll begin."

Their first afternoon was an experiment, a test shoot. Except for her sandals, all her clothes stayed on. Ruthie was embarrassed by the tracks left by her dirty feet, but Nathan didn't get mad. She was a little girl, he insisted.

He coached her—chin down, eyes up, mouth slightly open. The slow movements and poses Nathan drew from her felt oddly familiar even on that first day. "A natural," he even complimented her, as Ruthie moved from one pose to the next.

For one of the first times in her life, Ruthie could feel she was good at what she was doing.

At the end of the session, after she put her sandals back on, Nathan trailed her through the center aisle of the sanctuary, promising her it was only the beginning of what they could do.

In the vestibule, she waited as he slid back the bolt and opened the door.

"You'll come back," he said. "I know you will."

When Ruthie stepped out of the dark building, the sun's glare startled her. It was as if she'd stepped out of someone else's tomb.

"Presents!" Nathan said as Ruthie emerged from the bathroom, switching off Christmas lights. He held boxes wrapped in white paper and ribbons.

"Nathan!" she said. Ruthie loved presents, even his, which were never for keeps. Everything he gave her joined his Collection. Tearing away the paper, she found white patent leather shoes. Two smaller boxes held thigh-high fishnet stockings and white elbow-length gloves.

Ruthie stood in front of a mirror, centering the back seams on the stockings. The rubber tops snapped around her thighs, making a bulge she didn't like.

"That's sexy," Nathan said.

"It's fat," she said.

"The chair," Nathan said. "This time we'll do it for real."

Ruthie made a face and reached into a bin of makeup he'd bought her—pinks and silvery lavenders—"fairy colors," he called them. She applied the pink lip liner and lipstick the way she'd read about in a drugstore magazine, following the natural vertical lines of the mouth with strokes and smudges instead making a disgusting clown circle.

Nathan watched. He never got angry, not even when she took forever doing what he asked her to do. As he watched, Ruthie turned and looked at her butt in the mirror. 103 pounds. Definitely improved. She put her hands on her lowest ribs, remembering shadows.

"The chair," Nathan said again.

"The chair never works," she said. "It's ugly. I don't want to look ugly."

"You'll like how these pictures turn out," Nathan said. "I promise."

Ruthie stepped onto the tarp. "But how will I see them if I'm leaving?" She opened her knees into a grand plié and lowered her hips, concentrating on keeping the fishnets away from the sharp metal joints of the chair.

"You'll give me your address," he said. "In Indiana."

Chest lifted, legs wide, Ruthie twisted her hair with both hands. She pressed her parts against the chair, rocking back and forth the way he asked her to do. Nathan still didn't pick up his camera. She kept rocking. She would make him pick up his camera. He even said it sometimes, she was making him do this.

"But you can't show anyone," he said. "They won't understand. People are afraid of beautiful things."

Don't tell. Ruthie remembered the picture of the Shroud inside the gardener's pocket.

"I'll forgive you," she said, rocking.

"I don't want forgiveness," he said.

"If people find things, I mean. I'll forgive you if they ask."

"They won't ask," Nathan says. "Even if they find them. They'll pretend they didn't see them. People are mostly afraid."

"The shoes!" she said irritably. "I forgot the shoes." She hated it when she did stupid things, especially stupid things other people could see.

Nathan tossed the shoes toward her. One … two … they landed on the tarp. She squished her feet into them.

"Up, up, up," Nathan said annoyingly.

She launched her hips off the seat and took a few steps in the heels. She circled the chair, sucking in her stomach. She glanced in the mirror.

"These shoes make my butt stick out," she said.

"That's good," Nathan said, but instead of taking pictures, he pulled a second folding chair to the edge of the tarp and sat down, facing her.

Ruthie stopped walking. She'd noticed he started taking fewer pictures during her last visit. She wanted to know why. Maybe because she'd lost weight. Maybe he envied her. Since she'd gotten skinny, other people treated her differently too. All at once, boys started looking at her on the street. Her mother commented on her improved profile.

Even though he wasn't taking pictures, Ruthie leaned heavily onto one hip. Maybe Nathan was jealous. She'd gotten skinny before his eyes!

"Enough," Nathan said, pulling a pack of cigarettes from his shirt pocket.

Irritated, Ruthie sat on the chair, legs closed. She despised how fat her thighs looked whenever she sat down.

"What will you do when I'm gone?" she asked.

Nathan lit a cigarette.

"You have a lot of souvenirs," she said, trying to be funny.

Once, he'd showed her a page of "proofs" from one of their shoots. Because he shared a darkroom with a biologist, a strip of pale white skeletons labeled *Platysternon megacephalum* had gotten mixed into the rows of her face, her body, and her hands holding her special parts in a special way.

"At least you'll remember me," she said.

"I'll remember you," Nathan said, tapping the end of his cigarette into a lens cap. He pointed his chin toward the Collection.

"Take something," he said. "I want you to remember me."

The shawl lay where she'd dropped it near the boxes and torn wrapping paper.

Nathan followed her eyes. "I know what you want," he said.

Ruthie could never take the shawl home. Rachel would find it. Or even worse, her mother would find it, ladylike and delicate among her little girl things, and demand to know where that sudden beauty had come from. Ruthie imagined her mother's words as she lifted the silk from her drawer: "What have we here? I spy something awry—"

Somehow, her mother's warnings always sounded like the beginnings of fairy tales.

"Take it," Nathan said.

Ruthie looked down. The insides of her elbows had begun to sweat under the lights, darkening the gloves. "These are stupid." She threw the gloves on the floor and kicked away the shoes. She peeled off the stockings, annoyed by the red imprints they left on her thighs.

"I've lost weight, Nathan," she said. "Can't you tell?"

He smiled. "Of course I can tell. I noticed before you did."

"Why didn't you say anything?"

He took a drag on his cigarette, staring at her. "Because you're already full of yourself."

"I'm not full of myself," Ruthie said. "I've worked hard. All summer." She lifted her chest. The camera hung from a strap around his neck. She would make him do it. She would make him pick up the camera.

"Vain," Nathan said, crushing the stub of his cigarette.

Ruthie lowered her chin. *Perfectly perfect.* She lifted her eyes.

"Vain," he said again.

Ruthie shook her head.

"Will you remember me?"

"No," Ruthie stared at the camera. "I've already forgotten about you." She arched her back and widened her fingers across her thighs. It scared her how much she loved the camera, how badly she wanted him to shoot. Little girls disappeared into grown women, he'd told her, but his pictures would last. He said his pictures would save her.

Nathan tossed the shawl toward her. It landed in her lap. "Take it," he said.

Ruthie opened the fabric and wrapped it around her body. She drew her knees to her chest.

At last, Nathan brought the camera to his eye. When he took pictures, he moved more lightly.

Ruthie looked back at him in a way he liked.

Yes . . . yes . . . yes, the camera whispered.

Taking pictures freed him, he sometimes said. Maybe she was saving him.

Beneath the hot lights, her scalp began to sweat. She pulled the shawl tightly across her face. The fabric stuck to her damp skin.

"People look at me now," she said.

"People look," Nathan said. "People always look."

Ruthie opened her eyes. Her mascara and lipstick had stained the white silk.

"Beautiful," she heard him say. "I made you that way."

Through the impression of her own face, Ruthie watched Nathan kneel before her.

You Can Be Madonna *If*—

THEY LEFT SCHOOL during lunch hour. He kissed her as they pulled out of the high school parking lot and turned up the stereo.

It was February in northern Indiana, and a storm had just added a foot of new snow to all that had fallen months ago. They tunneled between dirty snowbanks that rose higher than the car. Patches of black ice dotted the road. In the passenger seat, Ruthie pulled the corners of a red-and-green plaid blanket around her shoulders while steadying the paper bag in her lap.

He kissed her again at a traffic light.

"Thanks for coming," Ruthie said.

"What's that supposed to mean?" Luke's voice was irritable. "Why wouldn't I come?"

"Thanks for coming," Ruthie said. "That's all I mean."

"So, what do you think? I'm an asshole?"

"Of course not!" Ruthie grabbed Luke's hand on the gearshift. "I love you," she said, even though she knew he wished he could leave her.

"We've decided," he said.

Ruthie shrugged.

"I mean, we're just kids," he said. He didn't look at her. "We're sixteen."

Ruthie stared out the front window. She didn't feel like a kid.

"We're too young to be having kids."

"I know that," Ruthie said.

Traffic started moving. Before he started the car forward, Luke reached over the gearshift and kissed her again.

Ruthie loved how the ugly city she'd known her whole life disguised itself like a fairy tale after a storm. Snow rested in the crevices of the trees, their branches glistening with ice. People skied excitedly down unplowed side streets. Even the ugliest houses looked like gingerbread houses, frosted with snow.

The next morning, everything would be gray and mushy and ordinary again.

Luke turned down the stereo. "What time was the appointment again?"

"Noon," she said. "I've told you three times now."

"And you gave them your name?"

"Yes."

"You gave them your real name?"

"Yes."

"You know you could have used a different name," he said.

"Why wouldn't I just use my name?"

"You didn't give them my name, did you?"

"Luke!" Ruthie closed her eyes. "I gave them my name. That's all."

"Okay," he said. She heard him fiddling with the radio again until he settled on a rock station from southern Michigan. "I'm sorry," he said.

Luke wheeled the car around the corner. Ruthie opened her eyes and pointed at a shabby house. The walk hadn't been shoveled. The drive was only half plowed.

"I think that's it," she said.

Luke pulled to the side of the road. "Are you sure?"

"There's a sign."

It was a house, but a portable marquee sign on roller wheels sat outside the door. Red block letters announced FREE TESTING above a phone number.

"This has to be it."

"You'd think they'd do a little more with it," Luke said, pulling the car as far as he could into the drive. He stopped under a large tree and switched off the music. As Ruthie began to crawl out of the warm blanket, a branch weighed down by heavy snow fell just in front of the car. Ice pelted the hood.

"Damn," Luke said as he opened his door. "That was close."

He took her arm as they went up the icy front steps. The only thing that made the place not look like a regular house was a sticker on the front door that said Enter. And below that, Entrez chez nous and then, Por favor, pasa. As if anyone spoke anything but English in their town.

Inside, a woman sat behind a folding table reading a book. A rotating wire rack filled with pamphlets loomed beside a shabby couch. The rest of the room was cold and empty.

"Welcome," the woman said pleasantly enough, though she didn't smile like most people Ruthie knew.

Ruthie stayed close to Luke.

"Do you have an appointment?" the woman asked.

Ruthie gave her first and last name. "I called yesterday."

The woman dragged her index finger down the list. She shook her head. "You used your real name?"

"I called," Ruthie insisted. She set the paper bag on the table.

"All I have today is a Madonna," the woman said. "And a Princess Leah."

Ruthie laughed but stopped because no one else did.

"Madonna," Luke said irritably. He touched Ruthie's elbow. "You told me you said Madonna. Remember?"

The woman glared at Luke. "You can be Madonna if you want to," she said to Ruthie, closing the appointment book. "It will only take me a minute to set up the lab."

"Jeez," Luke said as the woman left the room. "Everyone thinks I'm an asshole."

"I don't," Ruthie said.

They sat on the couch. He put his arm around her and held her the way she liked to be held.

"Are you okay?" he asked.

Ruthie nodded.

"Because we don't know anything yet."

"We don't." She pulled his hand even tighter around her shoulders. "I'm cold," she said.

"You're always cold," he said.

"Madonna," the woman called out loudly when she returned, as if others were waiting there.

Luke stood with Ruthie.

"You're coming too?" the woman asked.

Luke didn't answer. Ruthie picked up the bag from the table. They followed the woman into a small room with a large desk, a television, and a folding chair.

"I guess I'll have to get you a chair," the woman said curtly to Luke. "Since you're going to be in here too." She left the room.

Ruthie sat on the folding chair. Her knees hit the desk.

"I don't like this place," Luke said. "For Chrissake, you can't even move in here."

The woman returned and opened another chair behind Luke. She went around the desk and squeezed her hands into latex gloves that snapped around her wrists. "I'll take the sample," she said. Beneath the latex, the woman's long fingers and almond-colored nails turned into long beige tentacles.

Ruthie gave her the bag.

"You did a home test?" the woman asked.

"Yes," Luke said.

"Yes?" The woman directed the question to Ruthie.

Ruthie nodded. It was a lie, but as of that moment, a lie she'd told twice. There was no way she could bring a test like that home. But it had been three months since she'd had her period.

"I'll take this into the lab. You can watch this while you wait." The woman turned on a video and flipped off the light. She went into a brightly lit side room divided with only a cheap shower curtain and pulled it shut. Through the thin plastic, Ruthie could see the woman's silhouette as she took the small canning jar filled with her urine from the plastic bag. She heard her unscrew the lid as a man with a familiar movie star's voice began to narrate the video.

On the monitor, they watched buckets filled with fetuses swimming in blood as the narrator gave "statistics" about the number of fetuses "disposed of" each day. A fast-motion sequence went through the developmental stages of the embryo.

"I feel sick," Ruthie whispered as the embryo sprouted into a three-month-old fetus in front of them.

Luke put his arm around her shoulders.

Ruthie looked away. Outside the window, she saw the upper branches of the tree in front of their car reaching toward the winter blue sky. In one of its crevices, fresh snow topped an abandoned bird's nest.

She glanced back at the video. The narrator continued over footage of a fetus squirming inside its mother's body. Ruthie decided she'd concentrate on the nest. She imagined three secret eggs inside. With her own X-ray eyes, she could see through their shells. Each one contained a tiny human fetus, growing like the one on the video. Their tiny fingers opened and closed. Their big heads pushed against the insides of their shells, their strange wide mouths opening upward like baby birds.

Ruthie concentrated so hard on the babies in the nest, she almost didn't hear Luke say, "This is shit."

"What?" she whispered.

The woman behind the shower curtain stopped moving, listening either to them or to the movie.

"This is shit," Luke said. "We're in the wrong kind of place."

"What are you talking about?" Ruthie asked. Luke was Catholic. He knew more about practical things.

"Let's go," Luke said, but he didn't move.

"Almost done," the woman said, busying herself again. When the movie ended with a tiny creature somersaulting contentedly to classical music in its crimson den, the woman pushed away the shower curtain and switched off the TV.

"Well?" she asked.

"We'd just like the results of the test," Luke said. "That's all we came for."

The woman walked behind the desk. "It isn't that easy."

"It is," he said.

"What's easy?" Ruthie asked.

"We'd like the results," Luke said.

The woman said to Ruthie, "I'd like to speak with you alone."

Luke stood up and put his hand on Ruthie's shoulders. "No way," he said.

"Madonna," the woman said, looking at Ruthie. "Alone."

"You're not talking to her alone," Luke said.

The cramped room was silent. Snow had muffled the whole world outside. When Luke moved his hand from Ruthie's shoulders and grabbed the back of her metal chair, the sound was unnaturally loud.

"This is ridiculous," Ruthie said. She turned to Luke. "Go on. I'll be fine."

"Five minutes," the woman said to Luke.

"I'll be fine," Ruthie said again.

"I'll be back in five minutes," Luke said to Ruthie. "Five minutes. I'm counting," he said to the woman as he shut the door.

Alone with Ruthie, the woman pursed her lips.

Ruthie smiled to be polite.

"Young lady," the woman said. "Consider your family."

Ruthie looked down. Her parents knew she wasn't a virgin, but she didn't want to think about them. "Is there a baby?" she asked.

"Dear," the woman continued more gently. "If you can't control yourself around boys—"

"I don't hang around boys. I only hang around him."

"I know who your father is," the woman said, but Ruthie didn't want to talk about him.

"I didn't get baptized," she said as if that explained something and put her hand on the empty chair. "Can he come back in? Now?"

"No." The woman snapped a fresh pair of gloves over her hands and went back behind the shower curtain.

The babies! She looked back at the nest. No one else knew they were there. Their open mouths pressed against the inside of their shells—the babies were waiting for her.

The woman walked back into the room holding a paper and sat behind the wooden desk. Winter light shone through the window, making the paper almost transparent.

"Is there a baby?" Ruthie tried to see through the paper. She wanted an answer.

"Dear." The woman set down the paper. "You don't realize how young you are."

Ruthie smiled. *Jealous!* The woman was old. She probably couldn't even have babies anymore.

"Not to mention, you are terribly thin—"

Jealous! Ruthie stood up so quickly she felt dizzy. That's why the woman didn't want to tell her.

"—you've possibly ceased ovulation."

Ovulation—even the word sounded nested with eggs.

"Tell me," Ruthie said, grabbing the edge of the desk.

"It's been five minutes." Luke opened the door. "It's been five minutes, at least." He stood next to Ruthie. "What did she say to you?"

"Luke." Ruthie smiled. "I'm fine."

"Is she pregnant?"

The woman opened a drawer and put the paper inside it. "We don't know," she said. "We can't tell from the test."

"You can't do that!" Ruthie said.

"What did she tell you?" Luke demanded, looking at Ruthie.

"Maybe it's too early to tell," the woman said. "Maybe, it's because she's terribly thin."

"It's been three months!"

"We want you to come back," the woman said to Ruthie. "Alone."

"We're leaving," Luke said. "Crackpot place. You people don't know anything."

Ruthie didn't move. "I want you to tell me. I want you to tell him."

"Tell me what?" Luke said.

"There's a baby," Ruthie said. "Somewhere. I know there is."

"You'll have to call us," the woman said to Ruthie. "You'll have to come back. Alone."

"There's a baby," Ruthie said again, staring at the nest.

The woman pointed toward a side door. "You can leave from this door," she said to Luke. "In case you don't want anyone to see."

"See what?" Ruthie said. She didn't think she understood anything anymore.

A woman they hadn't seen before entered the room with their coats. "You'll be leaving from here?"

"Jesus," Luke said as they put on their coats. "Yes, we're going. We're both going."

"Call us," the woman said again to Ruthie as they walked through the side door onto the snowy steps. Luke took her arm and helped her make her way through the snow down the drive. Luke opened Ruthie's door, and after she got inside, he grabbed the blanket and wrapped Ruthie up as tight as he could. He tucked in the ends and kissed her.

"That lady was full of shit, Ruthie," he said. "You know that, don't you?"

As he went around the car to the driver's side, Ruthie looked at the tree. The nest wasn't visible as they sat inside the car, but Ruthie knew the babies were there. She could feel them.

Luke started the engine. As they waited for it to warm up, he said, "What did she say to you? That's what I want to know."

"Nothing," Ruthie said.

"I hated leaving you in there, alone with her." He kissed her on the forehead. "I hated that more than anything."

Ruthie stared at the tree. The babies were there. How could he not feel them?

"I can't go back to school now," he said. "I can't think about anything. Let's go to the park." He began to back the car out of the driveway, away from the tree.

She felt something tearing away from her. "Luke!" she shouted. "Stop!"

He slammed on the brakes. "What! For Chrissakes, what?"

Ruthie stared at the tree. "I can't . . . get that movie out of my head."

Even if he knew the babies were there, he wouldn't want them. It was the best she could do to keep him beneath the branches for a little bit longer. She just wanted him there.

"That movie didn't mean anything, Ruthie." Luke slid the parking brake on and searched through the blanket for her hand. "Those ladies are nuts. You know that, don't you? It was one of those places that pretend to be a real place. Just our luck," he said. "I hate this town."

Ruthie stared at the branches.

"Look," he said. "I'll still pay."

"She told me to stay away from you," Ruthie said. She started giggling. She didn't know why.

Luke pushed her hand away. "What's wrong with you?"

Ruthie kept smiling. She put her hand on her stomach, even though she knew it would upset him.

Luke hit the steering wheel with both fists. "We don't know anything yet."

"I know that," Ruthie said.

"I can't marry you." Luke put his hands over his face.

"I know that," she said.

"I don't want to," he said.

Ruthie nodded. She looked back at the tree because it almost sounded like he was going to cry, and she'd never seen him cry before.

"I don't love you," Luke said.

"I know that," Ruthie said.

Foragers

EVERY TUESDAY AND Thursday afternoon, the girls met on the second-floor balcony of the public library at their favorite table next to the two-story window overlooking the street. Cold wind pressed against the glass as each girl arrived, wearing coats under coats, mittens under mittens, heavy turtleneck sweaters, and, buried far underneath, two layers of socks custom made by a local needle champion known for her perfectly turned heels. Her tightly knit masterpieces had become a secret emblem for their club.

In the girls' minds, the table on the balcony was their very own. It had exactly five chairs—a sign! The table was meant for them. They'd come to expect it on those afternoons, demanded it when necessary, and the librarians acquiesced, cowed, the girls believed, by their unyielding demeanor. They were, after all, very good girls who knew to whisper in libraries. They never giggled or sang. They never brought boys. They were self-sufficient, requesting assistance only when necessary.

"We never use the word 'help,'" the girls agreed.

Their favorite librarian knew which books the club needed—large reference volumes with detailed plates and illustrations—always the same books. On slow afternoons, the librarian even had the books waiting on their table. The other librarians sometimes scolded her for encouraging them. "Why?" the girls heard them say.

Their librarian was curious and perhaps a little jealous, the girls decided.

"She wishes she could be one of us," Ruthie said.

The girls smiled around their table. The librarian could never be one of them.

Initiation into their club had been a silent process. Each girl recognized herself in the others. Their shadowy habits were the same. At school during the terrifying shuffle between classes, they were the girls who crept close to the walls to avoid the stray arm or backpack that might bump or bruise their refined bodies. They were the girls who turned away from people they'd known their whole lives.

Everyone watched them. Everyone wanted to interfere. They were the skinniest girls in school.

Every Tuesday and Thursday at their table on the balcony, each girl set out a calculator, a spiral notebook, and a silver water thermos— no history of contamination!—purchased just for those afternoons. Together, they filed to the drinking fountain, where each girl watched the next fill her thermos to the same line. No member was allowed the satisfaction of knowing she had the least water weight inside herself during their meetings.

Other patrons watched their procession. Periodical readers gazed up from the floor below. Returning to the table, the girls set down their thermoses, opened the books, and began.

First, they consulted a coloring book for students studying anatomy that contained black-and-white line drawings of the human body neatly divided into subsections and systems. Assigning these sections and systems among themselves, the girls turned to more complicated volumes and medical books that identified parts and organs in Latinate terms printed in microscopic fonts that made the girls feel like scribes divining codes from mysteries begun long ago. Adding the weight of each organ, the weight of each bone, the mass of each muscle, the club searched for the body's purest weight: the perfect minimum.

Equations, facts, and diagrams filled their notebooks. The female encephalon: forty-four ounces. Spleen: seven ounces. Each ovary: one to two drachmas. The club adored the organs willing to downsize along with them: "the combined weight of both kidneys in proportion to body weight is 1 to 240." The heart stumped them with its riddle: it grows heavier throughout life, resulting in a proportion of 1 to 149. But how heavy was the heart at their age, seventeen?

Melinda began with the Digestive System, teeth to rectum, and, on completion, advanced to the Organs of the Senses: nose, eyes, the labyrinth of the ear, the tongue. Susan worked on the Great Groups of Connective Tissue, including cartilage and bone. She complained the most. Scientists were always leaving things out, avoiding specifics, and wasn't being specific their very job? Some sections and parts were described with no mention of weight at all!

The girls shook their heads. Even the scientists were against them.

Lisa Simon, a former math champ during the days when grades mattered, tried to determine how each member's skeletal frame might affect her perfect minimum. She assessed their proportions—this girl shorter, that taller—in combination with bone density. But when she asked each girl to divulge the exact measurement of her wrist, they all refused.

They knew Lisa Simon was jealous. Lisa Simon was the biggest in their club.

Along with her investigation of the Female Organs of Generation, Ruthie coordinated the project, tabulating their results in a yellow notebook. She made sure no member hoarded information for herself.

Angelica, the skinniest member of the group, sat next to the window.

Ruthie didn't make her do numbers. Angelica simply observed their diligence with a distant smile.

Calculations and numbers filled their pages as they worked through the winter. Snow banked and drifted around the maple saplings in the parking lot across the street, but the club still arrived, never mentioning the shocked stares of faraway relatives who invaded their lives during the holidays and tried to interrupt their routine.

Though they were girls who often caught colds—girls who teachers didn't expect to see at school anymore—no member ever missed a session with the club. What if the others learned something? Found the secret? Got ahead?

In February, they returned to the knitter's studio for new socks to reward their perseverance and to help them remember at all times that they were chosen—a club.

The woman shuddered when they explained why they needed extra pairs. Not enough fat left on the bottom of their feet. Their heel bones pressed too sharply against their soles, pricking the inside of their skin. On that same visit, they asked the knitter to embroider on each ankle an ancient Greek line drawing of a pomegranate they'd found in a library book.

"An insignia," they begged. "A special symbol meant only for us!"

To their surprise, the old woman refused. "Girls, girls," she said, grabbing Ruthie's bony shoulders in her hands.

On the second-floor balcony of the library, the girls all indulged Angelica. A delicate presence with enormous blue eyes and a pale frizz of hair, Angelica had popularized fainting spells at school. In her seat beside the window, Angelica sat motionless for hours or focused intensely on drawing skeletal human figures. The club admired Angelica's drawings, though one disturbed them—a detailed silhouette of the female body filled with tiny circles.

Cells, Angelica explained.

The implication of those circles overwhelmed them. So many numbers, so much work still ahead!

Other times, Angelica told stories. In the story they loved most, a specialist told Angelica she fascinated him. As her mother watched, he made Angelica stand naked in front of a full-length mirror. She shivered as he brushed his fingertips across her bare collarbones.

"How do you do it?" the specialist asked.

In the mirror, Angelica saw her mother begin to cry.

The girls nodded around the table. They all made their mothers cry.

The specialist touched the reflection of Angelica's eyes. "Tell me," he said. "What do you see?"

The club listened with envy. Angelica's eyes indeed set her apart. Her eyes seemed to grow larger by the week as her cheekbones sharpened below them. They too had wondered, could Angelica see something more? As they worried over details, foraged through facts in pursuit of one number, did Angelica know a simpler truth she hoarded for herself?

Angelica was the skinniest, and they could all see she was getting even skinnier!

Finally, Angelica offered a hint. They'd read the facts aloud at that very table. Animals, when nearing their minimum, lose peripheral vision. Their minds rule out distractions. Nothing exists but the hunt. They see only prey in front of them.

"Human minds are the same," Angelica insisted. "My peripheral vision is gone."

The other girls nodded, anxious for the day their minds would free them from distractions, when even their sight would get skinny!

Tracking her eyes across each face at the table, Angelica said, "Prey. I see nothing but numbers in front of me."

Angelica was the first to be taken away.

On the first Thursday in March, Lisa Simon was late. As the club waited, sunlight gleamed across their table and reflected off their empty silver thermoses. Though they never spoke of Angelica or took her empty chair, each girl wondered whether Angelica was still holding out, restrained, as girls sometimes were, to a hospital bed with an IV unit dripping calories into her, counting butt squeezes and tiny stomach crunches beneath the white sheets, making contractions so small no one monitoring her could see?

During sleepless nights, each member prepared and practiced such things.

Lisa Simon still hadn't come. The girls filed to the fountain, filled their thermoses, returned to their table, and began.

Halfway through the session, a car drove into the parking lot across the street. As Lisa Simon ran toward the library door, the club saw her pretty stepmother get out of the car and look toward the upper part of the window.

"I'm sorry," Lisa Simon whispered when she reached their table.

The club kept working.

Lisa Simon wanted to explain. That day in school, a boy in her physics class, a boy they'd all known forever, had walked toward her desk while the teacher was out of the room. He must have forgotten no one talked to them anymore. Had they noticed? People only stared and whispered about them now.

The club concentrated on their books and numbers. Lisa Simon was speaking too loudly. She was ruining their reputation. They were, after all, very good girls who knew to whisper in libraries. They no longer wasted their time with silly boys.

Lisa Simon went on. That boy said he could see she needed help. It was obvious, he said, that she needed things. Everyone in this town is on something, he'd whispered. He offered to get things for her. For them. The club.

The other girls kept working. They pretended they hadn't heard the numbers cheapened in that way, their project dismissed as a passing phase, a self-absorbed game. They knew other people blamed the influence of fashion models, foolish girls who were cheats in their eyes. It was easy to be skinny with such long legs. Those girls needed cigarettes and drugs. Those girls needed money and fame. They needed help because they got skinny for other people. Those girls didn't understand the inspiration, the purity, or the discipline of the numbers.

No one understood. They—the club—were like no one else.

"I told," Lisa Simon said.

The club looked out the window. Lisa Simon's stepmother was still there. She was looking for them. Angrily, the girls turned back to the project, to the safety of their pages, to the safety of the numbers that would never betray them.

"I'm sorry," Lisa Simon said again.

Lisa Simon was the biggest in their club. She was not one of them.

Lisa Simon was the next one taken away.

In April, as the club worked on the balcony, a group of popular girls and boys from their school entered the library and took a table in the periodical section on the first floor. The club leaned closer to their numbers, but they couldn't block out the sounds of those boys. They heard boys slapping each other on their backs, boys telling jokes, boys laughing with each other, boys laughing with pretty girls among the newspapers, chairs, and tables.

The club worked even harder.

One boy jumped on a table below and began stomping. He shouted back at a patron who stood up and complained. The popular boys and girls laughed harder. Other patrons turned to watch.

Even the club stopped their work. Susan went to the metal railing that edged the balcony and looked down to the first floor. Her movement caused one of the girls below to look up. She pointed. The popular kids all turned. The other patrons looked to see what had silenced the room.

Everyone stared at the club.

It was a test! The popular boys and girls were sent to test the club's allegiance to the numbers. Ruthie opened the yellow notebook and began to recite from their collected facts. "Fat is first detected in the human embryo during the fourteenth week," she whispered.

Fat. Fourteenth week, Susan and Melinda recorded in their notebooks.

The kids below began laughing again. They laughed louder and louder and continued to laugh as one of the librarians escorted them through the front door.

"Thank goodness," Ruthie said after the library resumed its order. She closed the yellow notebook. "Thank goodness those children are gone."

Susan and Melinda nodded, though they all watched the popular kids walk down the street, the stupid boys with their stupid arms around the stupid girls.

"Those kids are always laughing," Susan said. "We never laugh."

Ruthie and Melinda turned back to their work.

Susan said she was sorry. She knew she was interrupting the routine, and the routine had been tried enough for one day. But she couldn't stop noticing how much those kids laughed. Their laughter distracted her more than their looks and stares.

Ruthie and Melinda kept working.

Susan went on. Were they even supposed to be happy? She needed to know because her family said they wanted her to be happy. They wanted her to take pills, Prozac or Elavil. Her family would never understand. There was no way to learn the calorie count of those pills. How would she know how many leg lifts and sit-ups were needed to cancel out the numbers swallowed with those pills? Doctors might even inject calories into them. How could she be happy if she couldn't do her equations? Her mind would never rest.

Ruthie and Melinda kept working.

Besides, Susan said, there was no time to be happy. Adding up the fat and calorie count of everything she absorbed, subtracting the expenditure of every activity, even walking—3 calories per minute—and breathing—15 calories per minute—the calculations and facts never ended. She memorized the calorie count of food she only looked at, of food she'd never seen. Things like shad—71.5 calories per ounce; and roe—40 calories per ounce.

Shad, they recorded in their notebooks, 71.5 calories per ounce. Roe, 40 calories per ounce.

And the project, Susan said. Didn't they know their goal was impossible? The eyeball, embedded in the fat of the eyes' orbit. Their tongues—fat, muscle, and nerves. Their fingertips, everything they touched was translated through layers of fat.

Eyeball embedded in fat, they wrote. Tongue—fat, muscle, and nerves.

Susan went on. Didn't they know their task was impossible? Even if they decided on the perfect minimum, could they imagine stopping? Wouldn't they still have to beat it? Wouldn't they still have to beat each other?

"I'm sorry," Susan said again.

Susan was the third girl taken away.

At their table on the balcony, Ruthie and Melinda continued the project. They even kept up the water fountain routine, though it seemed ridiculous to them now. Ruthie knew Susan was right about the project. A minimum wouldn't allow them to stop. What were they without the pursuit of the numbers? What were they if they couldn't watch each other?

One afternoon, Melinda put down her pencil. She pulled off her socks and stood. Her face flinched as her heel bones pinched the skin of her bare feet against the cold floor.

"Each night," she whispered, "I make myself walk. One step for each number. I want my body to feel each pound that's left."

As Ruthie watched, Melinda walked slowly along the edge of the balcony. Sunlight streamed through the two-story window, illuminating her narrowed face and the remaining fluff of her hair. She gripped the metal rail. Her fingers—knuckles, tendons, and bones—echoed the anatomical drawings in the books on the table.

67. 68. Ruthie counted each step. When Melinda stopped, she smiled. Both of them knew. Melinda was the skinniest.

Smiling still, Melinda rose onto her toes. She pulled herself onto the rail and leaned farther over the periodical section. Was Melinda threatening to take that easier, obvious way out, to cancel the numbers? To steal entirely the chance to get ahead?

Ruthie yanked open the yellow notebook and searched for an entry that described how bones, when starved, begin to stockpile fat in their marrow. The club had read the facts aloud. As they got skinnier, their very bones would sabotage their efforts, hiding more and more fat in their innermost recesses. Ruthie would remind Melinda it was useless to cheat in that way. She would only land in pools of her own fat that had long been preparing, waiting to thwart her.

But when Ruthie stood to read the passage aloud, Melinda was gone. There was no disturbance in the periodical section. Had the numbers called her back? Smiling, counting, feeling each number left, Melinda must have walked to the stairs and crept her way down, away from the project and away from Ruthie.

Melinda was the fourth girl taken away.

The next Tuesday, on the second-floor balcony of the public library, Ruthie sat alone. Their favorite librarian had set out their books. The librarians, the patrons, who would notice first that the other girls had disappeared? Where are your friends? Ruthie expected someone to say. She would explain the project, its clear objective, and the organization of the data. The idea was mine, she would say. Because hadn't everyone been watching? Couldn't everyone see?

She was the skinniest girl in school.

Ruthie opened the yellow notebook and wrote: I win. I win. I win.

The Order

THE WOMAN HELD the present against her chest as her husband
adjusted the long seat behind the wheel of their fifteen-year-old station
wagon. She'd paid extra to have the box wrapped in gold paper she
hoped her daughter might love, a silk flower for the top even, and now
it was getting ruined in the rain. After the seat fell into place with a
rusty click, the woman slipped inside the car with a tired joke about a
similar sound in her knees.

Her husband didn't respond.

She pressed her fingertip against a damp wrinkle in the paper as her
husband backed the car out of the drive and onto their street, shadowed
beneath the gnarled overhead grip of late-winter sugar maples.

That morning, she'd called the hospital and confirmed their daughter's status. Their last trip had been made in vain, the painful drive endured only to learn Ruthie was in solitary confinement and on bed rest again after she'd pushed the staff to the limit with the polite refusals the woman knew well. Though she and her husband sat for two hours on the overworked blue couch in the waiting room, the nurses wouldn't even inform the girl her parents had come.

"Procedure," the floor supervisor curtly explained.

She'd reacted in her tearful and furious way, informing them it was quite obvious to anyone that their daughter, along with all those self-centered starvelings surrounding her there, *wanted* to disappear. Her husband's grip had tightened on her arm as her words grew sharp.

How could solitary confinement improve anything? These sorts of girls would simply believe they had won.

The incompetence of the staff, their inability to unlock the mystery of their daughter's mind, infuriated and terrified the woman. It drove her to this point where she could do nothing but focus on a white open space she dreamed up behind her eye sockets. But on this day the sensation only disturbed her.

Dry heat blasted into the car. The woman spoke to her husband immediately.

"It always rains when we go. Have you ever noticed that?"

He shrugged and stared at the road. She saw that he'd spread his overcoat across the back seat before they got in and then turned on the heater with a force that nauseated her. At a traffic light, she wiggled out of her raincoat and maneuvered it onto the back seat, smoothing it across his. She put the box on her lap again.

On the drive from Elkhart to South Bend, all that could have gone wrong did just that. Every traffic light turned red immediately in front of them. On Mishawauka Road, a detour nudged them three miles out of the way at a ridiculously slow crawl behind a car with an angry gray dog trapped behind a hatchback window. The quivering beast barked with soundless fury.

Staring through the window while doing nothing made her restless, but when she reached over to tuck in a tag that stuck out from the back of her husband's sweater, he caught her hand, held it firmly for a moment, and then pushed it away.

Her husband, eloquent and warm in front of Mennonite congregations and ministerial forums, spoke so little when it was only the two of them. Sensitive, he was in too much pain. His silences made her self-conscious about those banal statements that came out of her mouth. Traffic. Weather. The insensitivity of friends.

Their daughter Rachel had left them too. She'd disappeared, taking only her violin. And though Rachel had been found, she still hadn't returned. Two bedrooms empty. In one short blow, her daughters taught her the difference between silence—that sacred ground—and sorrow.

She looked at the car in front of them again.

The dog was staring back at her. Without warning, the creature threw its body against the window, pressing a single dark eye against the glass, teeth bared.

Her mind froze.

The dog started barking.

The woman looked away and asked, "Will Ruthie allow us to see her this time?"

Her husband shrugged instead of answering her.

She looked down. The gold paper was beautiful even in the gloomy light. Perhaps Ruthie, even if she refused to see them, would accept the box and hold it in her hands just as she held it now. The woman imagined Ruthie's fingers pulling at the ringlets of gold ribbon, wrapping the silk flower behind her ear to enliven her remaining blonde hair. Perhaps Ruthie would even think of her that very afternoon as they made this same dreary trip home.

Her husband startled her with a sudden gesture over the steering wheel, one he made frequently behind the pulpit, as if he'd just been sent a message to deliver from that dreary sky.

"What are you thinking?" she asked too eagerly, a question he hated, but, even after eighteen years, she remembered too late.

"What?" he asked, startled out of his reverie. "What?"

She'd done it again.

The pretty shop girl who helped her choose the shiny paper had looked seventeen, Ruthie's age. The woman found herself asking for more and more—this kind of ribbon, please . . . tied in that kind of bow?—just so the shop girl wouldn't leave. The flower, stiff petals with a long gold stem, had been the girl's suggestion. As she wrapped and secured the paper and slid the blade of a scissors down the ribbons to make them curl just so, the woman found herself grateful almost to tears for that pleasant attention, no matter how routine the transaction had been.

At the hospital, the station wagon swung into the garage and wound up five levels as they searched for an open space. When they stood beside the car to put on their coats, her husband leaned forward to brush the back of her blouse.

"Chalk?" the woman wondered out loud. "No. It must be flour. Miriam hugged me in the bakery just this morning." Her husband shrugged, but she appreciated with her whole being that brief contact. His touch puffed her up a little for the disappointments—she knew she shouldn't feel this way, of course—that were invariably coming. She tightened the belt around her waist and picked up the present, circling it with both arms.

Rain matted the woman's gray hair against her scalp. As they waited for the light to change at a crosswalk, the hospital loomed coldly in front of them until her husband cut it o-ut of their view with the decisive pop of an umbrella.

They waited in silence, avoiding the truth neither could speak aloud: their daughter was growing worse. Though they'd seen Ruthie only once in the two and a half months since her arrival, weekly reports showed numbers, routine vitals—a weakened heart conserving energy, sadly slowing its beat down. Highlighted in yellow, they'd watched their daughter's body weight slip below numbers the woman remembered Ruthie passing years before as a child.

How could a mother let her daughter grow so thin?

The woman opened her coat and slid the box under her coat, pressing it against her chest. She looked up and counted the rows of windows on the awful building, determining what must be the fourteenth floor. Ruthie's floor.

She envisioned the others around her, gaunt, expressionless girls shivering beneath their long robes, shaking their heads at the world they'd left behind. Creatures made of air. Evil spirits. *They'd enchanted her child!* And right at the time when others her age were coming to the front of the congregation for baptismal water from her husband's hands. Only Ruthie chose not to. *They'd stolen her child.* She was losing her daughter, to *them*.

Her husband touched her elbow and guided her across the street.

A man in a suit jacket whose entire job was to greet visitors nodded as they passed through the enormous doors and stepped onto the red velvet runner that muffled the sound of their feet on the marble floor. They were never quite prepared for the elegant expanse of the lobby with its efficient attendants. Each time they entered, she felt as if they were checking into a hotel far beyond their means.

Yes, the stay, the bills, all beyond their means. But wasn't a daughter worth it, even if the child wished to sever the connection?

As they passed potted palms and other expensive displays, make-believe gardens made of flowers ridiculously out of season, the woman tried to calm herself with a meditation, one scrap of a prayer. But prayer seemed impossible there, pushed out by the clinical minds that ran the place. How easily they believed everything could be explained away. She had realized quickly after Ruthie's arrival that everything about their quiet and practical beliefs—to be in this world, not of it—would be reduced to an oppressive reserve, a misunderstood withdrawal, a certain link to their daughter's demise.

But Ruthie had checked herself in. Did they even have power left to take her away?

The woman smiled politely as her husband checked in at the hospitality desk. It was the Japanese receptionist, a pleasant young woman with sleek bobbed hair who was never patronizing.

"A beautiful box!" she exclaimed, drawing a neat pink fingernail down a golden petal. She briskly called up to announce their arrival and directed them to the elevator, as if they didn't stand in front of the same one each week, one of the few that opened on the psychiatric ward on the fourteenth floor. Even that was a lie. The Catholic hospital didn't believe in the number thirteen. What cruel quack had thought to put patients who possibly didn't know where they were on a fourteenth floor that wasn't even a fourteenth floor?

In the elevator car, a handsome young orderly dressed in white twirled a set of keys in his hand, his eyes fixed on the silver doors that shut tight in front of them. As they rose higher and higher, the woman wondered why these strong-bodied orderlies never spoke. *If orderlies were ordered not to break the order of the order.* Smiling at this lively nursery rhyme nonsense that had jumped into her head, the woman looked up at her husband and smiled.

"What?" he said irritably. "What?"

She looked away. Her jokes like this, little "trifles" he called them, came only during difficult or horribly real times and annoyed him.

They stepped off the elevator. As the woman and her husband waited for the floor supervisor, the orderly turned and opened the first in a series of unassuming doors that led to the locked half of the psychiatric ward. How much easier it would be if their daughter were in that cordoned-off otherworld, if an overzealous chromosome or too much fire in the brain could be faulted and blamed for her strange terrors. Other parents would sympathize with them—no questions asked.

Selfish thoughts! The woman squeezed her eyes shut. Such thoughts were about her own pride. Their daughter had the capacity to recover. She and her husband had hope. They were parents with hope. Ruthie might choose life. Their daughter might turn around and live—with or without them.

The floor supervisor who greeted them was a nurse they disliked, thick arms and beetle eyes lost in a dough-colored face. "Ruthie?" she demanded.

They nodded.

The supervisor looked at the gold box in the woman's hands. "What's this?" she asked.

"A present." The woman looked to the floor, at once ashamed and proud of the extravagant wrapping. "For Ruthie."

The nurse came around to the front of the desk. "Is it her birthday?"

"No," the woman said as the nurse took the present out of her hands.

"We are required to know what's in it. Procedure," the nurse explained. "Security. Things you wouldn't even consider . . ."

The woman couldn't look up. What sort of mother would give her child something she could hurt herself with? Her competence in question, yet again—but then, no. It was logical, a perfectly reasonable regulation. It was only that she hated how these minds believed they knew everything about their girl, knew everything about them. Their family had always been so careful, so private, showing only what was appropriate.

But now this world full of strangers had files—had discussions even, about them.

What she wanted most, the woman realized, was something private between herself and her daughter again.

Her husband and the nurse waited for her to pull herself together. Even he didn't know what the box contained, a loosely knit sweater that reminded her of a cocoon. She knew it was necessary to be strong, but at that moment it took all she had to focus on the dull gray linoleum her daughter stared at endlessly—her life suspended thirteen stories aboveground, comfortably out of touch with the real world, away from them.

Her husband cleared his throat.

The silence was unbearable.

On the other side of the nurse's station, slivers of young girls flitted back and forth in terrycloth slippers, their weightless bodies moving in and out of doorways without a sound, crisscrossing in the halls. She'd seen them. She knew they were there, standing in front of windows, staring down at the world they'd left behind. And other daughters confined to bed would be reading feverishly, not with the hope of bettering their futures or to satisfy curiosity, the woman knew that. These sorts of girls read only because they believed an active brain burned up more calories on bed rest than a passive one.

Silent, deceitful girls, a secretive order, they'd been waiting for her daughter all along. How had Ruthie heard them from so far away?

The woman said, without looking at her husband, "I'd rather not tell you."

The nurse nodded and carried the box to the phone. The fluorescent lights reflected in purple streaks down the metallic paper as the nurse spoke into the receiver.

The woman had no doubt that everything about her request would be recorded in a log after they had gone. The staff would concur—this mother knew the rules. Rules were rules. The rules had been explained months ago. "Mother attempted to manipulate," they would write in their charts. "Mother determined to get her own way." "Gold paper, ribbons, silk—mother preoccupied with beauty, with looks."

She'd ruined her own child.

Both children. The doctor's advice not to tell Ruthie that her twin sister had left home was easy, too easy, to follow.

In front of them, the nurse nodded into the phone.

"Dear," her husband began, but stopped as a soundless and fast-moving daughter darted into the reception area. She glided across the floor in thick socks and furry purple slippers, the ends of a hospital gown fluttering about her ankles. One had somehow got out! She hovered close to them, trembling, and then slipped away, smiling as if that breakout were the first movement she'd been allowed in days.

"Okay." The nurse turned around, unaware of the spirit that had gleamed in and out of the room. "We just need to inspect the contents after she opens it. Before she takes it back to her room."

The woman nodded, though even this win was an acknowledgment of defeat. They knew Ruthie would refuse to see them. The staff likely predicted there would be nothing to inspect. The nurse even smiled as she returned the present.

No, the woman scolded herself. They were being tested. This was a test of their faith.

Always, Ruthie gripped their hopes in her hands.

"I'll escort you to the visiting lounge," the nurse said. She opened the door.

They followed her wide hips into a long hall. The girl in the purple slippers had slid down a wall to sit on the polished floor, her head bowed between her knees. Another girl darted silently from one open door to the other. At the far end of the hall, two of them stood, staring out the window.

They stepped into the lounge, where they would wait on the blue couch as they did every Tuesday, knowing their daughter was five doors away.

Her knees cracked as she sat down holding the box in her hands.

"I'll tell Ruthie you're here," the nurse said.

"Tell her we have a present," the woman said, and then wished she hadn't. Her tone was too eager. Her husband even reached over and put his hand over hers on the top of the box.

With a curt nod, the nurse stepped into the hall and turned toward Ruthie's room.

Ordered by the order of the orders. She couldn't bear it.

She removed her husband's hand and carried the box to the window. She pressed her forehead against the glass. The view below was dull—a park without swings, a thawing duck pond the same awful color as the sky—but this was Ruthie's view. Ruthie's room was on the same side of the hall. She wanted to share it, this one small thing, with her daughter. Her husband cleared his throat again.

The previous evening, she had gone into Ruthie's bedroom on the second floor of their house. She'd slid her hand down the white eyelet bedspread, just as she would rub her daughter's back, if the girl would ever let her touch her again. As she sat, she heard the neighbor's grey-hounds barking across the street, their metal chains ringing and scraping across the pavement. She pushed the ruffled white curtain aside and saw them, dodging in and out of the light. Their ribs heaved in and out. They snapped at the air, their long chains continually crossing. How did those animals not kill each other?

The memory of her own hands yanking the curtains shut startled the woman in the silent waiting room. She caught her breath—*their daughter was dying here.*

She turned around. "We're taking Ruthie home," she announced. "We're taking her out of this place. Today."

But her husband only stared. He stared at her as if *she* weren't quite right.

"What?" she said. "What?"

Her husband's mouth opened, but he had no time to answer as a spirit floated into the room.

The woman gasped. The creature smiled. Tendons showed in her neck. Her cheekbones were covered in a fine down. This wasn't Ruthie. Though they hadn't seen their daughter in months, the woman was certain—this one wasn't theirs.

Where was that horrible nurse when they needed her?

Without a word, the creature reached for the box, but the woman held on.

"Dear," she heard her husband say.

The ribbons trembled as the woman stepped back. The gold paper split open beneath her fingers. She wouldn't let go. *This one wasn't theirs!*

"Dear," her husband said again.

Faith Is Just Another Sorrow

Sweet the Sound

And the sirens shall sigh because of you and weep.
—ENOCH 96

HE'S BLOCKED THE MOTEL door with furniture so Ruthie can't get out.

Not that she's tried.

He lies naked across the foot of the bed.

Ruthie sits at the head, on the pillows, fingering his trumpet. Blue light from the TV makes her naked body, his naked body, and all the naked bodies in the porn magazine he made her buy for him at the airport look softer. More pure.

"You owe me," he says, beginning again what has become their only conversation. He says she tried to kill him. She doesn't understand why she can't let him go.

Ruthie pushes the horn valves down in what she believes is a D-flat.

"I'm tired," she says. "I'm tired of all this." She waves toward the stack of furniture. "It's crazy. Two years—I still don't know you. You don't know me. We know each other less than when we started."

"Ruthie," he says.

Ruthie puts the mouthpiece to her lips, not because she intends to blow on it, but because she knows what she just said isn't true.

"I'm the best friend you have."

"You don't know that," Ruthie says, terrified that he does.

She stands up, walks across the flowered bedspread, and holds out the trumpet. "Play," she says.

He shoves the magazine onto the floor, stands beside the bed, and takes the horn with both hands. He presses the mouthpiece against his lips. Tiny muscles near his temples move as his mouth puffs up with air.

"Great Is Thy Faithfulness." The hymn blasts through the cheap room.

It could be ten o'clock at night or three in the morning. When Ruthie picked him up at the airport in Wichita, the sun had already chucked itself over the prairie's horizon. Since then, all they'd done was check in at the motel and make the most of each other before sleeping back-to-back like old marrieds for God-knows-how-long.

When she woke, he was barricading the door. First, she watched him. Then, she got up and made the bed the way he liked it, military style.

"Great Is Thy Faithfulness" he goes on.

Ruthie hears the words to the song, though no one sings them. She anticipates the highest note, as if the warbling old soprano from her home church, the one who refused to accept it was time to give up, could somehow follow her around.

"When you were a *real* musician, you closed your eyes," she says over his playing. "You felt the notes. You didn't just play them. You played from the inside—"

"You're right." He lowers the trumpet. "Just a pilot. That's all I am now."

He walks toward the closet where the uniform he'd been wearing when she picked him up hangs inside a garment bag. His pilot hat sits above it on a shelf. He puts on the hat. Underneath it, his blond hair, short even by airline standards, glistens over his skull. He turns back to face her. A set of metallic wings over the bill catches the light.

"You're right," he says again. "I'm out of practice. Will you sing?"

"No."

"You used to."

"I'm not going to sing just because you tell me to."

"You still know the words."

"I'm not a kid anymore. I don't have to sing just because I'm told to."

"Nineteen? You're still a kid. You just don't know it."

He shakes his trumpet violently. Drops of saliva ooze down the bell and slide onto the carpet. The sight of his spit makes Ruthie feel sick.

He goes on. "Remember that county airfield in Indiana?"

"What of it?"

"Remember how we crawled between the blue lights and the red lights and lay in the grass?" He smiles. "We were so close we could feel the vibrations of that little Saratoga as she took off over us."

"Remember we got fevers from the dew?"

"We got fevers from the cold," he says. "You can't get fevers from dew. We got cold because you didn't want to leave. You would have laid there all night waiting for the next plane to fly in. That was when you couldn't bear to let me go."

"I would have. But that was before—"

He steps closer. "Before what, Ruthie?"

Ruthie opens her fingers across a large pink flower on the bedspread.

"Say it, Ruthie."

"Play," she says.

He lifts his horn to his mouth. "Great Is Thy Faithfulness," he starts again.

When they met in northern Indiana, she'd just gotten out of the hospital for starving herself, for trying to starve belief out of herself, as if faith were a tapeworm that could be yanked out. He was flying a private jet for a small-time televangelist and playing trumpet during offerings and the Call, when worshippers stumbled down the aisles toward the front to claim, reclaim, or re-reclaim Jesus as their God-Almighty Savior. His copilot was the sax man. *Fools for Faith* was their band's name. With *Fools for Faith* scrawled across the back of their matching flight jackets, the pilot and the copilot flew the televangelist all over the Midwest, playing gospel and picking up Christian girls.

She still remembers how he looked on the stage. Like someone who might take her away from things.

Those "holy-rollin' days," he still says, were the best he'd ever known. But then those days ended. Because of her. Because she tried to kill him.

The pilot drops a note. Then another. He pulls the trumpet from his mouth and glares at it, as if it betrayed him too.

For months after he accused her of trying to kill him, he got panic attacks. Even during routine flights, he'd stare at the dash, uncertain what to do next. His copilot reported him. He was temporarily grounded because of her. The televangelist accused him of losing his faith, quickly found another sky-licensed Fool, and demanded the flight jacket back too.

When he started flying again, he had to go commercial. No bands. No crowds. No God, as if she had taken that from him too. Better pay, but ordinary. Sellout, he calls himself now, but he still refuses to fly anywhere without his horn.

Ruthie thinks of him sometimes, playing lonely praise songs from hotel balconies in Bangkok or Berlin. Or cheap rooms in Wichita. Like this one.

BAM!

A slam on the other side of the wall makes Ruthie sit up straight.

The pilot stops playing.

BAM!

Ruthie hears a man's voice, "I've got my little girl in here!"

The presence of someone else makes the room feel too real. The pilot lowers his horn. Ruthie pulls a pillow off the bed and covers herself.

Everything around her feels cheap. The bedspread smells cheap. The tables and chairs and lamps stacked against the door look cheap. The rubbery blackout curtains, the awful seams in the awful wallpaper— she's suffocating inside *cheap*.

"These rooms," she says. "They're too quiet."

"Quiet is good," he says.

"Quiet makes me feel dead."

"Quiet is good. You're just too young to appreciate it."

"I'm not a kid. You don't know me at all anymore."

"I know you, Ruthie." He stares at his fingers on the horn's valves. "I know your body."

"So do other people now."

"What's that supposed to mean?"

"Nothing."

"Nothing?" He shrugs. "It doesn't matter. I've known your body longer."

"What does that mean?"

"I know how your body's changed."

"It has?"

"Of course it's changed. You were even more of a kid when I met you." He smiles. "Don't worry. I like it."

"I'm not worried." She hates how her voice sounds. Like it needs something. "Just tell me how it's changed."

"It doesn't matter."

"You loved me because I was so skinny I looked like a child. That's what you always said—'you look like a child.'"

"You still look like a child."

"'Blessed are the children,' you used to say."

"You still look like a child."

"I still look like a child . . . is that why you come back?"

"No." The pilot smiles. "That's why you need me."

Ruthie wants not to care. But something small inside her makes her ask, "If I still look like a child . . . how has my body changed?"

"It doesn't matter. What matters is that no one *here* knows you like I do."

"You don't know me now."

"I know you, Ruthie. You change places. You get confused. You think you're a new person when all you are is the same person in a new place."

"You go different places every day."

"But I don't let myself think places change me. I'm a pilot. I'm solid that way."

"You never change," Ruthie says. "That's for sure."

"Neither have you. That's why you need me. I know who you are, even when you're in a new place."

He walks to the window and pulls back the blackout curtain. Green light from the parking lot spills into the room. "What's so great about this place, anyway?" He waves toward the field behind the parking lot. "Did you even know prairie reads like the ocean at night? No landmarks. No lights. Only wind. Only currents. Only," he stops.

"Only what?" Ruthie sits up. Maybe he hears them too. Maybe he hears the sirens. In the prairie. At night. "Only what?"

"Nothing." The rubbery curtain clunks as he lets it fall. "Nothing but nothing out there."

Ruthie sits back.

"But you like that. You like it here."

"Yes."

He steps away from the window.

"It was a statement, not a question. I was just saying, you like it here."

As he goes back to his bag, he moves through the room without looking in the mirror. Ruthie noticed this when she first met him. How, when they walked through the glass corridors of airports or when he stood in front of mirrors in rooms like these, he never even glimpsed at his own reflection. Maybe after so much time spent staring through cockpit windows, he'd detached himself from the effects of reflective surfaces and mirages, trained himself to see straight through such things.

She envied that a little.

He pulls a white cloth from his bag, sits in a chair beside the TV, and starts polishing the brass bell of his horn.

"Now I will ask a question. Why do you like it here? In Kansas."

"I have a job here."

"You've had jobs before."

"But this one's in a garden place."

"A garden place?"

"We grow plants. Indoor and outdoor things. We transplant seedlings to eight packs. They're so fragile. But underneath they have these little roots you can hardly see—"

"And?"

"And we grow flowers. Roses, even. Miniature roses, no bigger than this." Ruthie curls her index finger to her thumb. "We grow them in all different colors. Black roses, even."

"Seedlings," he says. "Tiny roses. This is what you've become?"

Something in his question makes her feel ashamed. In the bell of his horn, she sees the reflection of her naked body and the reflection of the cheap contents in the room swirl together. She's trapped in a whirlpool of cheap.

"Last spring, we raised entire greenhouses full of geraniums. Cardinal Reds. Fantasia Whites. Me and a kid named Eden spent hours watering them. You should have seen it. In the morning, the sun made rainbows in the mist from our hoses." She laughs because she knows what she just said sounds stupid. "That's how my life is here. Acres of rainbows. Acres of flowers. How they used to promise us it was like to walk through heaven—"

"You work in a garden with a boy named Eden?"

"He's from Chiapas."

He stares at her face. She knows he's trying to decide whether she's making things up.

"You work at a place that gives jobs to illegal immigrants? Illegal immigrants and runaway kids."

"I'm not a kid."

"What kind of garden place is this, Ruthie?"

"I'm not a runaway."

"You're running away from your life. You're running away from looking at things. From believing in things. I know you, Ruthie. I knew you then. I know you now."

She holds up the bedspread. "Did you even know these flowers are hibiscus?"

"That's why you like this place? Because you can tell people the names of flowers?"

"I know more than their names. I know why the shape of their leaves matters. How roots have hair just to hold on to things." She lets go of the bedspread. "And the prairie. Did you know you can hear the prairie?"

"Ruthie."

"Sometimes you can hear it sing."

"Ruthie."

The sirens. He doesn't hear them. She can tell. "I have friends here," she says. "What kind of friends?"

"Friends."

"Garden boys named Eden?"

"Friends-friends. I don't know what 'kind' of friends."

"But your friends-friends don't know you like I do. You just think they're your friends because you think you can hide things. You think you can hide who you are."

"That's not true."

"Bring your friends with you next time," he says. "Bring Eden. I'll tell him everything I know about you. Then you won't have to hide things. You won't need me anymore."

"I don't need you now."

"Don't you always call me?"

She turns toward the wall. Her life feels small and impossible. Again. He goes on. "You call me because you need me."

The mattress creaks. She can feel him crawling onto the bed, creeping toward her.

"Ruthie," he says, "if you'd been with anyone else—"

"I was a kid then."

"It was last year."

"You made me fly."

"You begged me to teach you."

He grabs her shoulders and presses her against the headboard. The headboard hits the wall and makes a cheap sound.

"You tried to kill both of us." She closes her eyes. *Cheap, cheap, cheap.*

Always when they're this close, whether fucking or fighting, Ruthie remembers the day in Indiana when they flew above the fields. She remembers how those miles stretched out below them, a quilt of yellows, golds, and greens.

The beauty below them made him want to play. He promised her she knew more than enough to fly on her own. He trusted her. He had *faith* in her.

She took the yoke.

He took out his horn. "For the Beauty of the Earth," he began to play as she flew the plane.

Then she heard them. *For the beauty of the earth*, the sirens sang as he played.

She gripped the yoke. It wasn't the first time. She knew what they wanted. *For the beauty of the . . .* the sirens called as they yanked the plane toward the golden fields below, toward the land so eager to absorb them.

In the cockpit, the pilot threw down his horn. She held on tighter. She could see he was yelling but heard only their voices. *This our sacrifice of praise*, she heard as they pulled her toward the greatest love she'd ever known.

But then the pilot's hands were everywhere-everywhere. He took her off the command. He worked with his feet. He righted the plane and pulled them back up. Gravity rushed at her chest. The sirens returned her to her body all at once. Noise swept in—the engines' roar, the pilot's shouting. She put her hands to her ears as everything went back to being heavy and loud and ordinary again.

Ordinary, like the pilot pressing her shoulders against the bed.

"I knew exactly what you knew. You knew exactly what you were doing. I barely got us back up."

Ordinary.

"I saved your life, Ruthie."

"You saved your own life. It had nothing to do with saving me."

He lets go. He gets off the bed and picks up the trumpet. "Amazing Grace," he begins. As he plays, the room turns a deeper hue. On the TV, a man walks alone down a black sand beach. It's night there too.

...sweet the sound... Ruthie hears the sirens sing. Only they can tell her what she's capable of.

"Two in the morning for Christ's sake," the man next door shouts. "I've got my little girl—a child—sleeping here."

The pilot keeps playing.

The banging starts again, this time on the door. The furniture stacked against it begins to shake. The lamps on the table rock.

The pilot keeps playing as the man keeps pounding.

"A child!" the man shouts.

I once was lost ... the sirens sing. Ruthie closes her eyes. She hears them only when she's with him.

From the next room, a child's cry spills through the bars of the pilot's song as the man bangs on the door.

But Ruthie can't worry about them. The sirens demand her attention. If she doesn't listen, they'll abandon her again.

As the man pounds on the door, the lamps stacked against the door begin to rock.

Ruthie jumps off the bed. "No!" she shouts. She covers her head. The lamps crash to the ground. *Too late.*

In the next room, the child stops crying.

"Don't move." The pilot kneels beside her. He puts his hands on her neck. He presses her face into the carpet. "Don't move," he says again.

She's always too late.

The stink of stale cigarette smoke fills Ruthie's nostrils. She hears pieces of broken ceramic clack inside the metal trash can.

"See that?" he says. "You could have gotten hurt."

Ruthie feels groggy. Her whole body aches.

"Stand up," he says.

She doesn't.

"Amazing Grace," he starts humming, like he can't let go of the song.

She can't imagine getting up from the floor, but when she does, she sees he's sitting in the chair, holding his white cloth, polishing his horn again.

She sits on the bed.

"And tomorrow," she says. "You'll just get on some plane. You'll end up God-knows-where."

"Pittsburgh," he says. "I fly into Pittsburgh tomorrow."

"You'll fly to Pittsburgh. I'll go back to the greenhouse. We'll go back to doing our jobs. We'll pretend everything is fine."

"Everything *is* fine."

"I'm tired," she says.

"You're always tired," he says. "Soon you'll wear yourself out here. You'll get sick of your flowers. You'll move somewhere else. You'll get tired there too. You'll call me again."

"You don't know that," she says, but she knows he can hear she doesn't even believe herself anymore.

"I know you, Ruthie." He sets his horn next to the television.

"I don't understand what I'm supposed to be anymore."

"You were raised to live in a certain world. You were given rules, rules that exist with people who believe a certain way. No matter where you go, you'll keep running from that world that doesn't fit you. That doesn't fit us. But neither does the world outside of that world."

"How am I supposed to learn how to live any other way?"

"It's too late."

"Why do we keep coming back to these places? Why do we keep coming back to each other?"

"Because we're from the same place. We're from the same place inside."

"What is that place?"

"That place you go when everyone around you believes something else."

"*You* live in more than one world. You go everywhere."

"But where I go, the rules are clear. The cockpit is all about rules. About regulations. About knowing exactly what to do and when to do it."

"Is that the truth or what you have to believe?"

"Sometimes both are the same thing. That's called growing up, Ruthie."

"And we're just supposed to step out into it?"

"That's called getting a life."

"Find some stupid way to go on?"

"That's called knowing what you want. Getting a real job. Not running from thing to thing."

"Do you remember the first time you flew?"

"I remember every flight I've flown."

"You can't."

"I do."

"I remember my first plane ride. My family flew to Asunción. I was such a kid. I believed God made the wings of the plane. I imagined workshops filled with stacks of wings. Some for birds. Some for planes." She stops. "Why is it sad to stop believing in stupid things?"

"It's not sad."

"Is being told untrue things a betrayal? Or is the betrayal my not believing in untrue things?"

"You lost your faith, you mean. That's called joining the world."

Ruthie longs, sometimes, to be that kid again, that kid who could believe in things. But in the mirror in front of her, she only sees a naked girl on the edge of a bed in a motel room surrounded by prairie, listening for sirens.

If she leaves him, she'll lose them too. Unless she runs right into them.

"I'm ready to go," she says.

"Ruthie," he says. The way he says her name, all gentle and nice, means he wants to touch her.

"I'm ready to go," she says again.

"Okay," he says.

He pulls back the table. He moves the chairs. He opens the door and turns to face her. Behind him, dust swirls beneath a streetlamp illuminating the parking lot. And behind that, prairie grass ripples like an ocean, though she can't see it.

The pilot nods as if he's proved something. "I know you, Ruthie. You'll always come back to me."

He picks up his trumpet.

Sweet the sound . . . the sirens sing.

He plays louder.

The sirens grow louder too. *I once was lost* . . .

Ruthie wants to disappear into the sirens' voices. She wants to disappear into the prairie that remembers it was an ocean. A dry breeze from the parking lot blows through the door, but nothing in the room is light enough to move, not even the edges of the bedspread.

All she has to do is walk outside.

What Mennonite Girls
Are Good For

"MAÑANA?" RAÚL SAID.

"Tomorrow," Ruthie said. She could practically smell Tecate through the phone line. "I wait for you," she heard as she shoved the receiver into its wall mount and returned to the living room, where her roommate, Bev, sprawled in front of the television.

"Refugee?" Bev asked. "Again? Don't know why you put up with that."

"He's lonely," Ruthie said.

"Get one of those Spanish boys at the restaurant to teach you how to say 'fuck off,'" Bev said. "That's what I'd do."

Weak, Bev meant, and Ruthie understood, but even if she had known those words in Spanish, she wouldn't have used them.

Bev raised the volume on the television. Fake tinny laughter from a comedy Ruthie didn't recognize filled the room.

Ruthie sat down. She didn't know what to do about Raúl. He was different, more sensitive than the others had been. And he always called twice, the second time drunker than the first, as if he'd sat in that barren apartment agonizing over what he meant to say instead of realizing she'd hardly been listening at all.

Until that morning, Ruthie had been looking forward to the two-hour drive west to Ellsworth County, where she planned to take pictures of the petroglyphs on Inscription Rock for a Kansas state history course she was taking at the Mennonite college.

She'd only taken the summer class to placate her parents, whose determined optimism about her future always made her feel worse about the fact that all she'd been doing in the two years since they moved there was two months of work in a greenhouse stuffing seedlings into peat pots before waiting tables at Hank's, not even the best truck stop in their town. By contrast, her twin sister, Rachel, an environmental studies major at the Mennonite college in Ontario, was off doing her part to save the planet by planting trees in Saskatchewan.

That morning, when she stopped by her parents' house to ask if she could borrow their truck to better manage Ellsworth's off-road terrain, Raúl had been standing there, his face still sweating from whatever day job the church had found for him.

"You should take Raúl along," her father said.

Raúl nodded, though Ruthie didn't know for certain if he understood.

Her father knew nothing about Raúl's late-night calls. Ruthie wasn't even certain how much of them Raúl remembered. "Tomorrow," her father said, the matter settled.

Ruthie's father was a minister at one of the local Mennonite churches participating in the Overground Railroad, a church-based action group that gave emergency transport to men fleeing state and guerrilla armies in Guatemala and El Salvador, men with enough violence in their lives to be given church-sponsored asylum in Canada. By the time the men—she learned early not to call them by that faceless sweep of a word, *refugees*—got to their nowhere town, they'd already endured some harrowing escape through Mexico and over the US border only to find themselves stalled in Newton, waiting for documentation to continue north.

Her father found them housing and odd jobs and, more than once, gave the single men Ruthie's number if they asked for it after meeting her. She never told him they called at night, sometimes drunk, the town's dull nights leaving empty hours for memories of their recent traumas to erupt. Stories tumbled into her ear. Towns massacred. A child's naked body abandoned beside a road. A colony of monkeys senselessly shot dead in a jungle clearing.

So sorry, Ruthie would respond. Or *can't imagine*. She knew they called her because she was one of the few people they met even close to their own age. And she was the minister's daughter. They trusted her.

"Don't tell your father" was how Raúl ended their few conversations. Ruthie was never certain if he meant his late-night calls or his drinking, but this didn't matter. For whatever reason—respect, she supposed—she never told her father about any of those calls.

The phone in her bedroom started ringing again with an urgency that contrasted with the stupid laughter on the television.

Bev smirked over her beer bottle. "Want me to handle it?"

Weak? Bev's disgust wasn't right, but as Ruthie went for the extension in her bedroom, she knew something in her own actions wasn't honest either.

The next day, Ruthie picked up her father's truck and drove down Main Street to the apartment, a donated unit, where most of the men ended up. She passed the railroad station and stopped in front of the row of dilapidated buildings just south of the tracks. After she rang the doorbell, she returned to the air-conditioned truck cab to wait.

Through the windshield, the day seemed bored even with itself. A swarm of starlings pecked mercilessly at an Asian pear tree. A man spit chew tobacco into a beer bottle as he leaned against the wall of the Legal Tender Saloon, the lone holdout from Newton's past as a rowdy nineteenth-century cow town situated on the Santa Fe Railway at the very end of the Texas cattle drives. Cowboys once drove herds from Texas and Oklahoma, loaded them onto cattle cars waiting at the station, and blew the money they'd just been paid in Main Street's bordellos, dance halls, and saloons.

Ruthie tried to imagine the wide, empty road crowded with stage-coaches and wagons, the bittersweet smell of horse shit steaming up from the dirt and sludge, the adrenaline rush of moneymaking, gun-fights, and brawls. Jesse James himself had supposedly shoved a knife into the wall of the Legal Tender and inscribed "JJ," the initials never verified but dutifully preserved by the bar's owners. Ruthie had seen the letters, two simple lines surrounded by others hacked into the wall by decades of drunks.

Now, one hundred years on, late-night drinkers staggering out of the Legal Tender squared off only with sober, fresh-faced workers arriving for early-morning shifts at the popular Mennonite bakery across the street, a nightly showdown between the two halves of the town.

Finally, Raúl emerged. Ruthie could see he thought it was a date. He'd slicked back his hair with gel and put on a T-shirt so fresh from its packaging a grid of creases showed across his chest. He wore oversized dress pants and large shiny shoes. Castoffs, Ruthie guessed, donated by a well-meaning church member. He didn't get that they would be driving through dusty fields, squinting at rocks. The worst part, though, was he thought it was a date.

Raúl opened the door. "Ruthie," he said.

The solemn expression the men on the Overground Railroad wore always made Ruthie realize how much people smiled in her town, regardless of genuine feelings.

She decided she'd return the greeting his way. "Raúl," she said grimly, without smiling.

Raúl looked startled.

Ruthie liked how not smiling felt. "Get in, Raúl," she said.

When she'd picked up the truck, her father had given her money for gas and a little extra to take Raúl out for a meal on the drive home. "Right, Dad," she'd said, accepting the money instead as a peace offering.

At the gas station, Raúl leapt out and went for the nozzle, his eagerness to do what little he could only exaggerating his vulnerability. This irritated Ruthie, as did her instinct to make him feel better. *You don't have to do that, Raúl!* she would have said before that day. Or, smiling, *Thank you, Raúl. So kind!*

Instead, she stepped out of the truck without even looking at him. The smell of gas irritated her. The starlings flocked in a nearby tree irritated her. The birds had invaded the town in murmuring, squawking swarms drawn by some innate and inexplicable passion to destroy the pear trees the Lions Club had planted down Main, one more attempt at local "beautification" that had obviously failed.

As she walked toward the cashier's station, she saw Peggy, another waitress from Hank's, standing at a pump. This too would have irritated Ruthie, except that if anyone had to see her with Raúl, it might as well be Peggy.

When Ruthie was close enough to hear, Peggy gestured with her chin. "What's that?"

"Nice way of asking," Ruthie said.

"So? Tell me."

"My father's friend."

"Don't see Daddy."

Ruthie shrugged. Though her father never asked her to keep his activities quiet, the Overground Railroad wasn't the kind of thing she told non-Mennonites like her roommate, Bev, or Peggy, and certainly not the conventionally minded customers and drivers who ate at Hank's.

Peggy yanked the nozzle out of her tank. "What do you think he tastes like? Hot sauce?"

"Tecate more like it."

Peggy laughed, surprised by Ruthie's sting. *You're so nice*, Peggy often teased during their shifts, mocking Ruthie's soft voice and gentle presence.

"You have a good time now," Peggy said, opening her car door.

Sealed inside the roar of the air conditioner, Peggy's thirteen-year-old son waved. Her husband—newly returned from military service in Kuwait sick, silent, addicted to computer games, and impotent, as all at Hank's knew due to Peggy's careless complaints—stared dully through the front window.

Peggy honked as she drove off, taunting Ruthie with a thumbs-up.

Ruthie looked back at the truck. Raúl had returned the nozzle to the tank and was washing the front windows, taking care not to ruin his new clothes.

Weak. Nice. Doing God's work. That's what Mennonite girls were good for. Ruthie went into the station to pay.

They headed west toward Hutchinson on US 50. To the south, parched yellow wheat fields unfurled toward the Oklahoma panhandle interrupted only by crops of fiercely green milo. To the north, there was the same.

An awkward silence dominated the truck cab.

Ruthie could feel Raúl waiting for her to carry the conversation as she did on the phone, but she wasn't going to do that anymore. She shoved her sunglasses onto her face. The glasses were ridiculous, movie-star big, but good at absorbing the prairie sun. And they made her feel sophisticated, despite her T-shirt and shorts.

Ruthie raised her chin.

Raúl turned toward the window beside him. He cleared his throat uncomfortably. He was attractive, small-boned with fine facial features, an elegant nose. Though the age difference between them was only three years, Raúl seemed much older.

She remembered the faith story he had given at the church just after he arrived. A girl Ruthie's age who was already making herself *useful* serving Mayan communities outside Chichicastenango had provided translation. Raúl had been a schoolteacher accused by both guerrilla and governmental forces of using his position to incite rebellion. Other teachers had already been disappeared. Only weeks before that church presentation, Raúl had arrived at his schoolroom and found it emptied, a blood-stained knife stabbed into his wooden desk. He fled the building, fled his town, and didn't stop until he reached Guat City. He didn't know if any of his students—*children*, he emphasized—had been killed on his account. He didn't know if the screams and gunshots he heard in his dreams were memories or imaginings made of his worst fears.

Raúl ended his story abruptly. As the translator caught up, Raúl stared at the back of the sanctuary so intensely, Ruthie turned, half-expecting to see the parts of his story too painful to share imprinted on the bare white wall.

In the truck, Ruthie turned on the radio. Only one station played on that stretch of the highway. The twang of country music guitars filled the truck cab.

"This music," Raúl said. "I like it very much."

Ruthie switched it off. "That's funny," she said. "I don't."

The storage compartment between their seats was filled with cassette tapes her parents bought during public radio fund drives, vintage seasons of *Prairie Home Companion* and *The Best of Fibber McGee and Mollie*. But those shows had the old-timey jokes her father loved and things forever falling out of closets, jokes impossible to explain to Raúl. The loud sound effects might even scare him.

Gunshots, she remembered from his story. *Children*.

She didn't want Raúl to turn into a basket case while it was just the two of them.

The road thudded beneath their wheels. Raúl gripped his pants and stared at the fields.

Resentfully, Ruthie launched into a story about the last time she'd been on that road. She'd taken a bus trip home from Chicago to

Wichita. The trip shouldn't have involved Hutchinson at all, but when the bus passed through Leavenworth, a man boarded carrying only a small paper bag. Instead of sitting in one of the empty rows like any *normal* person would have done, the man chose the seat next to hers.

"Leavenworth." Ruthie glanced at Raúl. "Leavenworth? Federal prison? Jail, that means."

He nodded. He didn't get it.

"You see, Raúl," she said. "He sat beside me because I have one of those faces. Nice? Nicer than I actually am."

He nodded again.

Deciding that she wouldn't care whether he got her story or not, that she would tell it to the end unless he figured out how to make her stop, Ruthie detailed how the man grabbed her box of Fireball candies and poured the whole contents into his mouth. Tongue fireball red—*disgusting*, she added—he ranted about the dumbass bus, the dumbass passengers, and the dumbass sunset hanging over the dumbass Flint Hills.

"The guy was kind of 'off,'" she said. "You know ... loco?"

Raúl smiled. He thought, perhaps, she was telling a joke.

Ruthie looked back at the road. Route 50 was heavily trucked by long-haulers running toward the Rockies. In the afternoon glare, she had to watch for real potholes amid the false, shimmering mirages of potholes. *Mirages of potholes.* If she had to choose a symbol for her own dumbass life, that would be the image that might explain everything.

"I'll stop telling this story," she said. "It's stupid, really."

"I like it," Raúl said.

This made Ruthie feel worse, but ahead there was nothing but highway, and inside the truck there was nothing but story, so she continued. At the Wichita station, the man from Leavenworth followed her off the bus. Assuming whoever picked her up would be equally *nice*, he pounced on her father and asked for a ride to Hutchinson. The man must have lived in the area at some point because he knew what everyone called the town.

"Hutch," Ruthie said sarcastically.

"Hutch," Raúl repeated so solemnly, Ruthie was startled. Was he making fun of her?

She went on. Her father agreed, of course, though driving to Hutchinson added almost an hour to their trip. Imprisoned in the back seat, Ruthie was subjected again to the man's rant, which improved—of course—before his male audience.

He started with heroics. He'd been a dog handler in Vietnam. But after learning her father was a Mennonite minister and remembering from whatever history he had with the place that Mennonite implied a pacifist faith, the man changed his story to one that showed how his military service led him to the "peacely-minded take." After watching his dogs go to death for each other, watching his dogs drag dying soldiers for miles back to camp, he decided love was the soul's organic state.

"To hate, to kill another soul, those acts the *body*"—in the truck, Ruthie drew out the word, imitating the man's accent—"those acts the body had to be taught. Those acts the body could not forget."

But when US forces pulled out, there were too many dogs to take home. Jungle disease, the soldiers were told. Eaten by the Vietnamese was another line. But the men who owed their lives to those dogs knew the truth. "Tell me, sir!" the man's voice shook as they drove through the prairie dark. "As a man of God, tell me. What good is it, learning how to love if we all just get put down in the end?"

Abruptly, Ruthie stopped telling her story.

It was insensitive. It involved a war and a lonely man on the run. But it was a story born from the rhythm of that very road, born of her father's kindness, his rigorous practice of love, the same centripetal force that drew both of them there. And Raúl hadn't told her to stop.

She skipped to the end. On the westernmost edge of Hutch, the man directed them to a sprawling ranch house, dark except for a security light beaming from the top floor. Grasping his paper bag in his hand, he got out of the car, offered her father a military salute, and started down the long front walk as if he was expected there.

But halfway there, he stopped. They saw his body stiffen. He knew they were watching. He knew they could see that no one waited for him. He'd underestimated her father's kindness, her father's infallible hope, his need to see that a door would open to welcome that man into some kind of light. Instead, the man's fierce humiliation, his lonely lie, pinned them all to that point until he ran off and leapt over a hedge into the prairie dark.

Ruthie stopped.

Raúl sat up, recognizing she'd ended her story. "Your father," he said, "Big soul."

Ruthie nodded. This was true. "Big soul," she said.

Her story had certainly been insensitive, but maybe this didn't matter. Raúl would hear what he needed to hear. He couldn't afford otherwise. He'd put all of his trust, his very life into the church's hands. The enormity of this terrified her. It was dishonest even. Raúl would think he could trust white people. He'd been forced to trust them. His apartment and church-sponsored jobs kept him from the cruel words she heard while waiting tables at Hank's or sitting beside Peggy at her son's Little League games—jarring, brutal words, thoughtlessly tossed, meant to inspire laughter.

Or perhaps Raúl had heard those things. From the men who stood outside the Legal Tender below his apartment or when he walked to the store at the edge of town, where church people who sponsored him wouldn't see him spending their money on beer, perhaps Raúl had heard hatreds far worse than she ever had to hear.

"Tell me, Raúl," Ruthie said. "Do you believe in God?"

He turned sharply.

"The hell you've been through? I wouldn't blame you for lying. You have to say you believe in God. To get the church's support. To get here. To stay *alive*, I mean."

Raúl's mouth tensed. Maybe he mistook her questioning for some sort of test, some Great White Test of Faith, or for yet another interrogation.

"It's okay if you don't," Ruthie said. "I'm not so sure I believe in God myself."

He stared at the dashboard.

"Forget it," she said.

He probably believed anyway. Perhaps she was arrogant, believing she could live beyond illusions. But the more illusions she shed, the lonelier she got.

"You now," she said. "A story."

"A story?"

"Una cuenta," she demanded. Let him do the work. Let him carry the conversation.

"A story." Raúl braced his hands on his thighs again and quietly, clearly said, "I had a wife. I had a child."

Ruthie gripped the steering wheel. The road before them had not changed. The dying wheat fields, those hadn't changed. The dust-yellowed horizon, that too hadn't changed. *I had a wife. I had a child.* That was Raúl's story. Much better told.

"Dondé vamos?" Raúl demanded, as if telling his story had ripped something from him.

Driving farther from the only town in Kansas he knew, away from his apartment and routine jobs, it must have seemed they were driving toward the kind of place where anything might happen. Ruthie recalled a church movie—was it *Romero*, set in El Salvador, or a documentary from a Witness for Peace presentation? She remembered soldiers leading village men into a jungle clearing, stealing their clothes before shooting and burying them in anonymous mass graves. She remembered the women searching for bodies, their hands attacking the land as if *it* had committed the atrocity.

Didn't Raúl know things like that didn't happen here? Or did they?

"I have to take pictures of petroglyphs," she said. "Drawings on walls. Made by native people—los indios," she added uncomfortably.

He didn't get it. She didn't blame him. The trip was strange, as was the country's romantic fascination with cataloging its *own* history of genocide. The topological map her teacher photocopied for her was wedged between the stick shift and his seat. She could have asked him to open it. She could have tried to explain the elevation numbers, the red circles identifying the location of the drawings, but the moment had grown big and stupid and complicated again.

"Look," she said. "We'll stop on the way home. We'll get dinner. In Hutch."

Raúl smiled. Ruthie did not.

A ravine hidden by a cluster of trees took her by surprise. They descended too fast. Deep and very real potholes broke up the asphalt. Ruthie shoved down on the clutch pedal but reached too late for the stick shift. On each side, the trees flattened into a green blur as the bottom widened like a mouth below them.

Raúl gasped. His knees slid forward.

Ruthie felt a cold, satisfactory calm. Though she wasn't always good at it, she liked driving standard transmission. It was physical—her hand gripping and yanking the stick shift, her bare thighs tense as her foot worked the clutch. Her whole body tuned into the engine's hum, her whole body listening, her body could even correct its own mistakes if she didn't think too much.

They shot out of the ravine as abruptly as they'd dropped into it, the road's flat expanse spooling ahead as if the incident never happened.

Ruthie shifted back into fourth and then fifth gear.

Raúl's thigh pressed against her fingers on the stick shift. She only noticed because he took a breath. As if he'd rehearsed all night for that ridiculous moment, he announced, "I-like-you-very-much-you-are-very-nice."

Nice. Before that afternoon, she might have smiled. *Thank you, Raúl,* she might have said, or even, *I like you too*—on account of the hell he'd been through and because, as he'd just told her, he had no one else. But she wasn't going to do that anymore.

In the awkward silence *he* had created, Ruthie acted as if he'd said nothing. He could believe in God. He could bare his soul all he liked. She'd kept his late-night calls a secret. She'd obeyed her father and brought him along. She. Had. Done. Enough.

Raúl sat back.

Ruthie felt a strange alertness. She felt alive. Was this what people got from being cruel?

Swiftly, silently, they continued west through fields that stretched toward enormous cities, those glittering, dreamed-up escapes, where people had possibilities and could take charge of their lives and weren't so haunted and hunted like people she knew. People like Raúl, whole families even, forced to uproot their lives again and again. People like Peggy, driving her husband from one VA doctor's appointment to the next while disappearing with an occasional trucker to "feel a little less dead." People like her father even, so haunted by other people's hurts, by pains he couldn't reach, pouring his love for this world into sermons he offered each Sunday morning to half-awake souls and then slipped into manila folders ordered by date and filed inside drawers marked DELIVERED.

She'd seen them, the oldest pages yellowed and crumbling, his words returning unused—like so much available love—into air.

The roar of a train engine blasted Ruthie from her trance. She shoved on the brake. The truck jolted to a stop. Raúl slammed his hands on the dash but made no sound. She'd shamed him with her silence. She'd made him feel invisible, but she would not apologize.

The engine blurred past, followed by a rush of freight cars, each one yanking the next. No crossing gates fell across that unpopulated stretch of highway, but she should have seen the train stretching along the wide-open plain.

She remembered a similar near disaster, another train streaming out of nowhere, only that time it had been night. She'd been driving back from the women's health clinic in Wichita with Peggy in the passenger's seat, months after her husband's deployment to Kuwait. Ruthie had loaned Peggy money she needed for the abortion. Ruthie had given her a ride. But instead of thanking her, Peggy only said that even though they made the same pitiful wages and cheap-ass tips, she knew Ruthie would have money saved. And she knew she could get Ruthie to offer it to her.

Nice. "You're one of them," Peggy said. "Doesn't matter how much you think you're not." After saying these words, Peggy gave in to her body's exhaustion, sleeping the rest of the way to their town, where Ruthie nearly got them both killed.

That night, no whistle blared. There was only a single, solitary light sweeping across the track. That was the first Ruthie saw of those night trains, swift and silent, with pristine wheels that flashed like silver as they pulled shipments of military equipment, tanks, and vehicles. In the path of her headlights, the tan-and-beige camouflage designed to infiltrate the Gulf's desert terrain looked pale and sickly, like ghost versions of the familiar jeweled greens made to invade jungles in Vietnam.

There were reasons, she supposed, why military trains traveled at night. Rights of passageway. Lower temperatures. Less visibility to communities, like hers, that might stage protests. And even after the Gulf War ended, those trains kept coming, carrying midnight loads from manufacturers to Southern ports and military bases.

What dark genesis spawned the first war? Had her father asked the question one Sunday morning, or was it some unspoken darkness hovering over generations? For from that war was begat the next, and from that war was begat the next, and on and on—no exodus, no way out—only ghost trains and railroads cutting through the country, delivering the next war already begun.

The last car passed. Ruthie crossed the track and continued toward Hutchinson, its low silhouette etched onto the western horizon.

In Hutch, Ruthie turned north onto County Road 14 and headed toward Ellsworth County. Raúl was either asleep or pretending to be. As they left the city, oversized grain elevators graduated into smaller ones. Houses and schools and shopping areas thinned into long stretches of cropland until those too gave way to grazing land beneath the endless sky. Somewhere an invisible border was drawn. To the west, tumbleweeds hurled themselves into the road during their season, clogging up fenders and clinging to fence posts. To the east, tumbleweeds did not exist.

Progressing farther away from Hutchinson, the prairie unraveled into even wider expanses. Open range. The truth was, Ruthie understood why the vet kept spiraling back to this part of Kansas. She would never fully leave its vast, indifferent spell, not entirely.

She glanced at Raúl. His cheek pressed against the window, sunlight washing down his ear and collarbone. No logic or faith could explain why she lived paralyzed by the privilege of possibilities ahead of her while he lived forever moving, forced to accept whatever opportunity opened.

My life is perfect, Jesús, a translator from San Salvador, one of the men who called her at night, shot back on the phone after she tried to express recognition of injustices done to him. Spurning her pity, Jesús insisted he wouldn't have his life any other way—without the people he'd loved, without the people he'd lost, without being forced to learn how little is missed after abandoning everything. Living with death as an everyday fact, his life had rid him of illusion.

"You don't know shit about your own life," Jesús said. "How can you pity me?"

Jesús was right. She didn't know shit about her own life, let alone theirs. Because of him, after that conversation, Ruthie began limiting her responses to the men. *So sorry*, she'd say if necessary. Or *can't imagine*.

You-don't-know-shit.

As they drove down that road toward Ellsworth, its veil of dust undulating across the hot asphalt, Ruthie knew too that the intensity she believed she felt when she first saw that image of the petroglyphs they were driving to see was only more evidence of that *you-don't-know-shit*.

Seeking to preserve "history" with two-dimensional photographs, as if one could interpret and catalog four-hundred-year-old etchings of soul. Searching for meaning inside other people's mysteries, demanding this even, without putting her own "white girl" existence on the line—there it was, that same *you-don't-know-shit*, proving her false, selfish, and imaginary.

"Informational drawings" her teacher called the Ellsworth petroglyphs as the class passed around a photographic copy of a stereograph taken by a guy working for the Union Pacific Railway. The engravings were small, covering an expanse only two feet high and nine feet wide, hanging over Mulberry Creek. Drawn by Plains Indians or maybe Pawnee, the colors, if there ever were any, had long faded. Other petroglyph sites from the same time period showed more artistic advancement.

But, her teacher said, the rushed, crude quality of the drawings in Ellsworth suggested they were made to convey a story, some urgent history drawn in transit by a people moving toward a new life.

In other words, *we*-don't-know-shit. Colors lost. Stories stolen.

Only shapes and silhouettes remained. Triangles represented tipis. Horses stood on long stick legs. A row of warriors holding shields that looked like bull's-eyes—soldiers with bodies made into targets—guarded a figure dominating the center, a sacred shaman or chief wrapped in death robes. Lines radiated from the skull. A current undulated from the mouth.

As Ruthie held the picture in the classroom, she felt cold. Did that current represent a serpent, river, or spirit, or some other collective line of soul?

The shaman's eyes had no pupils, only a hollow stare absorbing a place far wider than the Great Plains, absorbing time beyond any transient human scene in front of it, far beyond the Mennonite students passing around pictures in an airless summer classroom.

Documenting the site would be "a service," their teacher told them. After four hundred years, the sandstone bluff threatened to slide into creek. Ruthie volunteered for the project that same day.

Ruthie glanced at the odometer. According to her calculations, the road to the petroglyphs had to be near. She slowed the car, searching for a break in the fence line. She saw a turnoff.

"Private property" a sign read. Then, in smaller letters, RUINS.

She made the turn. Gravel popped against the bottom of the truck bed. Dry, loose dust made the uneven wheel ruts almost slippery. The truck lurched as she shifted the engine into four-wheel drive.

Raúl sat up.

"This is it, I think," she said. Gripping the wheel with both hands, thighs tensed, she felt as if she was driving a horse through an open field of low-lying grasses.

A red pickup sat catty-corner across the lane. As they neared, Ruthie made out the silhouette of a man carrying a hunting rifle, walking toward the truck. An enormous dog moved alongside him. The slant of afternoon light exaggerated the length of the dog's legs. After they came into view, Ruthie realized that the man was motioning for her to cut the engine.

She did.

As the man secured a hunting rifle on a gun rack crossing the back window of his truck cab, the dog turned, eyeing them.

Ruthie glanced at Raúl. He sat very straight. Sweat beaded his upper lip. He hadn't spoken since he'd made his confession, *I-like-you-very-much-you-are-very-nice*. This realization pained Ruthie.

"It's nothing," she said. "He'll tell us we're in the wrong place. Or, if we're in the right place, he'll let us go on."

With the air conditioner turned off, the day's heat pressed against the truck. Ruthie rolled down her window. Hearing that movement, the dog raised its head, legs tensed, and pressed its paws into the ground.

The man herded the dog inside the cab, its skinny limbs reminding Ruthie of the horses' stick legs in the photograph of the petroglyphs. After the man slammed the door and started toward them, the dog lifted its head again, its bark sealed behind the window.

"Private property," the man said when he stood beside their truck. "Mine."

Ruthie took off her sunglasses and held out her student ID card. "We came to see the petroglyphs. For a class."

Ignoring the card, the man peered inside the cab, the brim of his hat shading the top half of his face.

Raúl stared at the lane in front of them.

"Who's the Sanchez?" the man asked, either assuming Raúl wouldn't understand the slur or not considering the term to be one.

"A friend," Ruthie said. "He's a teacher." Her face tightened into its habitual smile. *Nice.* She said too cheerily, "Hear you've got a real sight back there. You outta charge admission!"

"Think I aim to sit here all day waiting on dollars?"

"No, sir," Ruthie said, unable to get rid of the stupid smile stuck to her face.

If she didn't get to see the drawings after coming all that way because she'd brought Raúl, she'd never forgive her father.

The man took off his hat and shoved his fingers through his hair. Face bared to sunlight, he looked younger than she'd assumed. Fixed first on them and then on the lane in front of them, his steady gaze reminded Ruthie of a landscape painter from Cottonwood Falls, a customer at Hank's Peggy disliked. She said he had the kind of stare that could bore straight through her chest and see right into her poor soul.

The man settled his hat back on his head. "Keep going. Road you're on here is the old Indian trail. Park your vehicle beneath the windbreak. Can almost see the drawings from there, but you got to cross the creek to get close. No matter. Water's low."

Ruthie nodded. "Okay if I take pictures?"

"Do what you do," the man said. "Just don't go into the cave. Whole site's near collapse. Don't want injuries. Lawsuit, neither."

"Got it," Ruthie said.

The man turned back. As he neared the truck, the dog began to jump from seat to seat, barking soundlessly inside the cab until it laid its chin on the dash as if offering its own head, an animal gesture of devotion Ruthie strangely envied.

As she put her sunglasses back on, she smelled Raúl's sweat. Damp circles showed beneath his arms. The air conditioner had been turned off during the conversation, but he hadn't rolled down his window. Too anxious, perhaps. This too pained her, but she held herself back. She would not smile at him or say, *Thank you, Raúl, for being so patient*, as she might have done before that day. To-be-kind. Or *almost there! I promise!*

Instead, she started the truck and turned on the air conditioner and tried to focus on the fact that the lane they drove on was the *actual* Indian trail.

They drove into the trees. She parked and got out. After driving for so long, the solid ground felt good beneath her feet. She smelled sunscorched dust mixed with the musty green scent of nearby wet ground. She moved her sunglasses to the top of her head. The afternoon light flickered through the cottonwood and aspen leaves. The ground sloped downward toward what had to be Mulberry Creek.

Ruthie turned back for her camera, resting on the old quilt her father stored in the truck cab. Raúl stared through the front window, his seat belt still fastened across his chest. He looked miserable. Ruthie pulled the strap of her camera bag over her shoulder. His disappointment could only demand her attention if she let it do that.

She slammed her door and started toward the ravine.

The image the instructor had showed them was taken in 1867. He'd told them that, in the century between, the people and animals drawn on the wall had been used for target practice by cowboys and scouts, a common, cruel pastime. After that, white settlers imitating the Eastern rage for "picnicking" made day trips to the shaded creek and etched their initials into the stone between the original images.

But even with this warning, Ruthie wasn't prepared.

The warriors became visible first, the bull's-eye in the center of each body entirely shot out. The shaman's body too was stained and blackened. Bullet holes forced open what had been a blank, circular stare, making tears, a sick stigmata. The current spilling from its mouth was cratered open by that same violence.

The truck door slammed. Ruthie looked back. Raúl stood at the top of the ravine. His white shirt stuck to his chest. His face was flushed. He looked miserable. At least he understood this wasn't a date.

Balancing on the wet stones in her tennis shoes, Ruthie crossed to the other bank and picked through the brambles along the base of the wall. Up close, the petroglyphs looked even more pocked and ruined. Too high to reach, the settlers and sightseers must have climbed up the wall to carve their initials, like those decades of drunks who stabbed their initials into the walls of the old saloon beside the scribbled markings of Jesse James, as if one could piggyback on another's immortality.

Ruthie heard Raúl's hard-soled dress shoes slipping on the wet stones behind her.

She started up the path that wound around the base of the sandstone and saw the entrance to the narrow tunnel behind the stone ledge that held the drawings. Like everything else about the site, the cave was smaller and less elegant than Ruthie expected, but reaching it offered the satisfaction of realizing one small goal amid the day's frustrations.

"Ruthie?" Raúl called.

She ignored him.

Too impatient to wait for her eyes to adjust to the dark, she stepped inside, using her hands to feel her way. She knew priests and priestesses and shamans once gathered in caves all over the world to offer their chants and prayers, believing the echoes returned from the dark were responses from the divine. Her own history included sixteenth-century Anabaptist pacifists. Like Raúl, they too had been hunted, considered enemies of the state. They too huddled in grottos to pray in their own way to their God where no one would hear them.

But pressed against the wall, Ruthie felt no urgency. She felt nothing holy. She hadn't even known she wanted such things. She felt only small and alone in a crumbling cave, surrounded by the mysterious nothingness of the plains.

"Ruthie?" Raúl stood at the cave's opening. He couldn't see where she stood in the dark. "I wait for you?"

That was when the first shot sounded.

Raúl's body tensed.

The shot was far away, most likely the rancher going after a ground squirrel or prairie dog or taking potshots at sparrows. But a second shot triggered something in Raúl. His stance changed. Sunlight outlined his fear, his body remembering God-knew-what.

"Ruthie!" Raúl hurled himself into the cave. Had he become war's fugitive again, both hunter and hunted, driven to protect? His body shoved hers hard against the wall. Her arms and shoulders scraped against the stone. Her bare knees smacked the ground. She landed on her side underneath his weight.

Raúl gasped.

"Get off me!" Ruthie said. The strap of her camera case dug into her neck. She feared she might choke. "He's not even close!"

A third shot sounded. Raúl's body trembled and went slack, his weight sinking into her body.

"Raúl!" Pinned beneath him, Ruthie couldn't move. She heard the slow trace of the creek. She heard wind blow through the leaves of the cottonwood trees at the cave's entrance.

Raúl lay still. His sweat began to soak into her shirt.

"Raúl?"

Ruthie's mind raced. Had his exhausted heart given out? Would he die on top of her? She would have to drag his body out of the cave and to the car. She would have to report the incident. She would be found guilty because she *was* guilty. Though of what she wasn't certain.

"Raúl!"

Her petty meanness haunted her. Raúl didn't know where he was. He didn't know why they'd come there. He'd done nothing except call her after he was told by her father he could. He'd done nothing except call her, when he had no one else. He didn't understand why she picked up the phone. He didn't understand *nice*. He'd trusted her.

She tried to inch her body forward. His weight sank, pressing her more solidly against the ground. Dust coated the back of her throat.

Raúl's body started.

"Raúl?"

He took a deep breath. He was alive.

Ruthie tried to crawl forward. She would pull them both out. But as her body shifted below his, she felt—or did she only think she felt?—his erection pressing into her hip.

Her body stiffened. She opened her mouth, but nothing came out.

Stranger in a strange land . . . Exodus 2:22. Yes, father. We are all strangers here.

Don't reject him. Don't make him feel unwanted. Yes, mother. Nice, nice, nice.

"Get off me," Ruthie said, but her words were so quiet, they sounded like words she might take back.

Raúl's mouth opened. His breath dampened her collarbone.

With force that surprised her, Ruthie shoved his body away.

Raúl fell back but made no sound. Had she hurt him?

Hand. Foot. Hand. Foot. Ruthie groped toward the sunlight. Hand. Foot. Hand. Foot. *Nice. Weak. Nice. Weak.* She stepped outside. The heat choked her. Dust stung her eyes. Mulberry Creek trickled. The strand of a spiderweb clung to her cheek. Somewhere a dog barked at the disgustingly ordinary afternoon.

Forcefully, she brushed filth from her clothes and the smell of his sweat from her skin. She didn't touch the sticky place where his mouth had been.

Hanging from her neck, her torn camera case gaped open. She pulled out the camera. At least the lens hadn't been scratched. But she'd taken no pictures. One more failure to add to the afternoon.

She heard Raúl's hard shoes slipping as he crawled toward the cave's entrance. Already, she dreaded their drive back to Newton. *Sorry, so sorry,* she'd have to hear him say through stupid, unnecessary tears. Or *don't tell your father.*

She pressed the camera's top button. The film advanced. That first picture—her scraped knee and shredded skin—was an accident. But with it, a realization rose, one new and ugly.

She could say Raúl attacked her. Her father would believe her. Peggy and the rancher had seen them together. She was white. She was *nice.* Society's thick, vile prejudice leaned toward her side. All she'd have to do is tell that old, worn-out story, and wasn't it even true? Raúl had followed her into the cave. He pressed his body into hers even after she told him to get off her.

Hadn't he?

Don't want injuries, the rancher had said. *Lawsuit, neither.*

Ruthie waited with the camera held to her eye.

Her second picture captured the top of Raúl's head emerging through the opening. She photographed him crawling outside. He was crying. Snot shone above his lip. He must have heard the shutter's noise, but he didn't look up.

It's okay! Ruthie did not say, as she might have before that day. Or *I know you only wished to protect me.*

She photographed his fingers covering his eyes, his trembling mouth glistening with spit, his white shirt yellowed with grit. *Evidence*, she could call it.

A gunshot sounded again followed by the dog's bark. Ruthie watched Raúl through the viewfinder. This time, he didn't respond. Perhaps he finally understood these were everyday American sounds. Senseless gunfire, echoes of bullets carried by wind.

Ruthie returned to the path, walking carefully on the loose stones. She crossed over the creek. On the other bank, Ruthie turned and raised the camera again. Through the viewfinder, the warriors and the shaman grew clearer, their mouths defiled, their eyes forced open by hunters and ranchers. She zoomed in. The initials cut into the sandstone grew sharper. A picnic site for white people, and wasn't that her with the camera in her hand?

Raúl came down the path. He stopped beneath the warriors with their bodies made of targets. The shaman's eyes stared at her with collective force. Her father's gaze had some of this. Big soul. His heart so ready to love, ready to be broken. Was that what made him so quiet?

Raúl stared too. Through the camera, she watched him open his mouth. He might see her more than she would ever have to see him, her father's words had taught her that.

But this story was hers. Wasn't it? For as one story begat the next and as that story begat the next, her story—made of guns, of war, of so much *whiteness*—would be believed.

Or was this too a mirage, a crumbling ruin, disappearing at last beneath the afternoon sun?

Prayer Song for Johnny Cash
(Who Stepped in to Save My Poor Soul)

UNTIL THAT DAY, I'd never met a man named Gilligan, and it's likely I never will again, but there he was in my section with a bad case of the shakes, ordering a pitcher of ice water and Breakfast Special #7. *Gilligan* was embroidered above his shirt pocket, so I knew he wasn't the owner of that red Peterbilt cab glistening outside the window. He only contracted for some trucking company, which meant there was no chance of his being my ticket out of my Seventh Circle. Kansas. Truck stop. Johnny Cash drawling out "Ring of Fire" over local radio.

Escape was all I looked for in a man then.

"Looker," Peggy said as I hustled Gilligan's order to Jailbait, our sixteen-year-old grill chef and the boy Peggy slept with off and on, despite her thirteen-year-old son and her husband, who'd turned funny after Gulf War Number 1.

"Not my type," I said. "See that stupid name embroidered over his stupid pocket?" *Gilligan*.

"Little Girl?" Jailbait waved my order slip in the air. "How's your 'looker' want his eggs done?"

Jailbait called me Little Girl on account of my stature and because, despite time wasted on a college degree, I was still dumb enough to lend Peggy that four hundred bucks we all knew I'd never see again.

"Think I'm clairvoyant?" Jailbait asked me. "They teach you them words in school? Clair-*voi*-yant. Means I know what everybody wants."

"You just think everybody wants you," Peggy said, still eyeing my Gilligan as she headed toward the door for a smoke. "Table swap?" she shouted to me, but I knew she was kidding because she had Mr. and Mrs. Duchess, dotty but always generous with tips.

"Ring of Fire," Mr. Duchess bellowed with Johnny Cash as Mrs. Duchess beamed. Eighty-nine years old and married seventy-one, the Duchesses smiled 24/7 because they hardly heard a thing. "Walking Miracles" their daughter called them when she wasn't trying to take away their car keys.

I returned to Gilligan's table with his pitcher of ice water. "Eggs?"

He stared out the window at all of our nothing but highway and prairie and Peggy—smoking her cigarette, her skirt riding the wind, knowing full well she was showing him everything.

Mr. Duchess kept hollering out his "Ring of Fire," though Johnny Cash was done.

"Over," Gilligan said, giving me a sick grin.

We were all sinking deep, and he knew it. I slammed down the pitcher.

With that, Gilligan seized my wrist. Fingers trembling, he traced those telltale pink lines I'd carved into my own skin. He started laughing. "*These* trap you here?"

In towns so small everyone knows your scars, it's easy to forget what's exposed.

"Hell," Gilligan said. "Made it here. Finally."

I fled to the kitchen, and when Peggy came back in, she swore my looker plain vanished, and she never saw any red rig coming or going. Jailbait threw out the steak he'd started, insisting he'd known all along Little Girl called in a false order just to torture him.

"Clairvoyant," he said again, as if the word might actually mean something.

Behind us, Mr. Duchess kept going on with his song, all of us circling, circling down.

But I was already walking out of the kitchen and toward the front door, believing Johnny Cash himself sent that strange phantom in a red Peterbilt cab just to warn me that days lost to sorrow, discontent, and regret can spiral smaller and smaller and knot themselves into forever and even take your whole life if you're not vigilant.

The Book of Ruthie

MARTIN ALWAYS STAYS with me. That's the first rule. I set the limits. That's another rule, because even after the perfect little fantasy is worked out on the phone, a gentleman asks for more. No one ever touches me. I don't break laws, it's not part of my nature, although I suspect Martin might enjoy watching some illegal action.

"Don't you ever get bored?" I ask as we pull off the interstate in search of a hotel north of Boston, our usual realm.

Martin shrugs instead of answering me, preoccupied with finding the place.

We glide down the exit ramp and roll beside a stretch of forest. Neatly painted houses with family cars parked in driveways appear in manicured clearings. "Hello, Suburbia," I say, half hoping it will answer me.

A hotel thick with colonial shtick appears when the forest ends, just as our gentleman du jour promised it would.

"Not bad," Martin says as we pull into the lot. "Didn't even know this place was here."

"We should remember it," I say. "For the future, I mean."

I dig through my lingerie bag for the silk rose I clip above my left ear in case a reservation's gone awry and I need to be spotted quickly in the lobby by a certain gentleman.

Martin opens his door. "You ready?" he asks.

I pull down the sun visor and peek into the mirror to fasten my fragile flower. "I hope this one's not boring," I say. "I'm really not in the mood for boring."

"Vámonos, Ruthie," Martin says, giving his door a slam. Always, before we go in, he gets this funny tone in his voice.

Drawing our dreamers through a discreetly worded ad headed *Fantasy Givers*, we work primarily in pictures and film, but I'm always game for adventure. I love props and themes. Martin hates to get involved in the show aspect of things—we rarely do a double bill, although he's been known to unleash a disarming Little Boy Blue.

Inside the lobby, Martin heads to the front desk as I wait beside a fountain. A porcelain replica of a pilgrim ship sits in a pool made bluer than blue over turquoise tiles. Three enormous goldfish, all finlets and fairy tails, dart through a porthole. Such tight, tasteless quarters, but they're clean. Someone around here cares about them, it seems.

This scheme was all mine, but Martin never had objections. It started with our wanting the same thing, a down payment on our very own place. We're so close I've picked one out, a modest bungalow on the west edge of town. Sided in sweet peace-of-mind lilac, my happy dream home has a sunporch with fancy skylights that let in all kinds of light. In my mind, potted palms already sit in one corner of the porch beneath Martin's long Belgian wind chimes. The bay window off the breakfast nook will bring out the best from my poor gardenia bush, which hasn't had sufficient UV to bloom in years.

A dime flies over my shoulder, nicks the prow of the pilgrim ship, and bounces off into the too-blue water. The biggest fish flicks her tail just out of the way.

"Martin!"

"You're supposed to make a wish," he says, already heading for the elevator behind a sweet little chambermaid, her hips swaying in a perky Puritan style I catalog for future gigs.

"I just want us to wish for the same things," I say. "That's all I wish for."

As we ride to the tenth floor, I put my arms around Martin's waist, thinking of wishes and fishes and how close we are to living in our very own home.

Everyone I know is making love or money on the side, sometimes both. I don't fault anyone for bending the straight and narrow, not even my Martin. We're all desperate for shelter from the indifference of this world. We all need more cover. Martin laughs when I talk about shelter. He says I use the word in made-up ways. Obsessed, is what he says.

"We're almost there," I say, planting my smile into his chest, as if we were riding our way up to some honeymoon suite.

"Ruthie," Martin says.

Martin's sleeping with a girl from his office. A young thing is all he will tell me. And innocent, no doubt. I was suspicious for a while—I know what my man looks like in love. Finally, I asked, and he told me the truth. I'm thankful for his telling me the truth.

When the doors open, we walk down a corridor toward the day's dream chamber. Three sharp knocks and our gentleman appears, jacket off, tie loose. A lawyer, he confessed on the phone, a bona fide veteran of make-believe.

Eyeing the flower above my ear, he says, "Fantasy?"

"Your one and only, Allan," I say, entering the room.

A colonial-style quilt covers a king-sized bed shadowed by a giant Paul Revere–style lantern, ready to light up one-nighters, honeymoons, and other unmentionable midnight rides. Allan's camera sits on a collapsible tripod. Two set lamps, rentals no doubt, hang from cheap stands and brighten a white sheet thumbtacked to the wall.

"I'm a professional," Allan says, assuming I'd admire his setup.

"I can appreciate a pro," I say.

"Can we talk first?" Allan asks, sizing up my unthreatening Martin, my shiftless chevalier, who takes his seat on the quilted spread.

"Didn't we work it out on the phone? You said a bareback shoot. No frilly under-nothings." Hoping to tempt him with my cachet of cliché tricks, I open my lingerie bag and give each girly item a flick, but our legal eaglet is not at all moved.

"I'm an artist," Allan says, like so many of them do. He picks up a notepad and goes on about lights, color scheme, and other shoots he's done. He wants high-contrast nudes in black-and-white. Long limbs. Long lines.

Bo-ring, I mouth in Martin's direction. I kick off my high heels. I pull off my dress.

True "professionals" are heavyset, walleyed men who carry high-end point-and-shoot deals, pay me extra to sign a written release, and reveal no personal information, which Martin says is because no one in this fantasy business actually has personal information, but I refuse to believe that's true. In my heart of hearts, I believe even our pros leave us as happier husbands, better able to make happier homes when they kiss their wives on their cheeks and tuck their children in bed as visions of my sugarplums dance in their heads.

Allan's still droning on, detailing "aesthetics" to justify his needs.

"For Christ's sake, Al," I say. "Just tell me what to do as we're doing it." I slide the rose out of my hair, go between the lights, and hit my starter pose, a classical Spanish diagonal. "Surrender to the moment, Counselor," I say.

Allan steps toward his tripod with a face full of sulks. Our gentlemen pay me to listen, and right now I'm not. He puts his eye to the camera.

Chin down, eyes up, I remember. Mouth slightly open, I give him my best schoolgirl smile. I move between each pose slowly, working the line of each movement through to my toes.

Allan smiles. Once the work is underway and they see how I do what I do, our gentlemen always relax. There's a passive quality to paying dreamers. Something in them wants me to run the show.

One of my favorite jobs involved an evangelical motorcycle gang on the Cape, charismatic Cruisers for the Lord who wanted photographs for a calendar to finance their mission. Wearing nothing but white lambskin shorts, I straddled two Harley Davidsons and folded my hands in prayer. "Hallelujah," I cried out. Looking down at those lights, those men, and my wide-eyed Martin, I felt like the Virgin Mother providing necessary closure for their Wholesome Threesome, their Trinity—Jesus, the straight center line down that never-ending highway, and a woman sweetly saddled in back.

Coming home that day in standstill summer traffic, I was telling Martin how powerful it could be, providing beauty and pleasure, enriching people's lives.

It was so hot outside, I must have gotten a little heady, too full of myself, because Martin yanked the car off the road. He came around to my side and pulled me out of my seat. He held me close, saying over and over, "Ruthie, you're scaring me."

Allan sidles left and right, catching all angles of my work. "You enjoy this," he says.

"I like making people happy," I say. Gentlemen do enjoy that particular response.

I proceed with an acrobatic sequence I call my *PhantAssMagoria*. I feel that good old adrenaline rush but hold back. It's surprising how little men actually want once a woman stands naked in front of them. A little strutting and eye work for the most part, broken up with the traditional hair toss. I push my breasts together and pucker my lips like I'm blowing a bubble.

The worst of our times involved a quiet little gentleman who wanted nothing to do with pictures. One of our repeaters, he wanted me naked, wearing only a pair of Italian stilettos, lip synching to Maria Callas as he conducted with a brass baton. The first time, Martin and I laughed out loud in the middle of that scene, which made the little gentleman cry.

What kind of Fantasy Givers were we, he demanded, if we didn't respect his desires, if we didn't help him believe dreams could come true?

At our last engagement, that gentleman forgot his recordings. Moving his baton to the vibration of that hotel's hum, he traced my silhouette, the downy hair on my arms lifting to meet the cold metal as it passed over my skin. His hands shook. When I looked up, there were tears on his face.

After that, I had Martin tell him to stop calling. It was beginning to break my heart a little.

Remembering Allan's *I'm-an-artist* fantasy, I introduce my Art Trilogy. "Arbus and Avedon," I say, giving him a sequence of apathy, snarls, and lanky profiles.

Allan makes noises of approval.

I drop to the floor for my "Nod to Mr. Wegman," a masterpiece of brevity created for one of our half-hour Humberts who preferred the pooch position. I turn my hips suggestively, donning a blank doggie stare.

Blossoming into a healthy first timer, Allan's face grows flush. I stay on the ground and transition into a quick one act, evoking my biblical namesake, the prophetess Ruth, whose ancient search for shelter sends her down to the threshing floor.

"Wherever you go, I will go," I say, reaching for my bored-eyed Boaz on the bed. How easy it is, how dangerously easy, to find oneself here.

Martin's face remains fixed. He dislikes this part of my act, this story of love and loyalty. This lonely echo of my childhood. This wandering part of me that does not include him.

I turn back toward Allan, who keeps shooting. Raising sheaves of imaginary wheat in my raised hands, I cry, "May the Lord deal with me ... be it ever so severely. Book of Ruth. Chapter 1. Verse 17."

I rush toward the end line that makes all my believers swoon, "Punish me. Punish me. Punish me."

"Interesting take," Allan says.

"Last line paraphrased," I clarify.

For our final segment, a tribute to the classical tradition, I crouch on the ground, an animal arch igniting my spine, inviting Allan to zoom in on my heavenly haunches.

"The Gymnosophical Sphinx," Martin says.

Infinitely alert, infinitely calm, I hold fast.

"Buck naked and complicated," Martin says, remembering his cue.

Allan puts down his camera. "I'd like to do film," he says.

Sphinxlike, I hold my pose.

"I'd like something live."

I remain.

"Film" is when a gentleman wants you to do yourself, to show a little "pink" as the pros say, which costs even more. Or, possibly, he'll ask to do himself while I watch, which is double more, and choreography has to be specific because nothing touches me. And Martin won't watch for anything.

I break my pose. "Film is extra," I say. "We didn't talk about that."

Allan nods.

Martin gives him the numbers. "Money first," he says.

I look away.

It's an argument that has us sleeping back-to-back at night. Martin likes money up front, the bills laid out on the bed, especially when the numbers go up. But I'm too much of a working girl. I don't like to see cash till we've earned it.

Allan complies. "The money," he says.

I wait for Martin's nod.

"You have a theme?" I ask. "Live action is always better with a theme."

"You pick the theme," Allan says, steadying the video camera on the tripod. "You know what you do best."

We begin with "Little Girl at the Bus Stop," an early composition.

Delicately pointing my pettitoes, I sashay in front of the camera, stop, and gaze into the make-believe distance. Pretending to see Allan for the first time, I pull up my skirt and wink.

Let the little children come to me. . . . Matthew 19. I don't say the words, but I hear them.

Martin winks back from the bed, which makes me smile for real.

"It's more powerful when I'm prepared," I explain after our first run-through. "The whole bus stop scenario really swings into place with the purple cheerleader skirt."

"Props," Martin insists, backing me up. Allan shrugs off the detail.

I segue into the "Miss X-rated America Interview Challenge," acting out the parts of three excited finalists while Martin interrogates me from his quilted lair.

"Bravo!" Allan shouts. Gentlemen always love little "Miss Pink" Tennessee.

"A court scene," I announce to our lawyer and bend on one knee, calling up a dialogue loosely memorized for a filmmaker's "Miller Fantasy."

"It was only sport at the beginning, sir."

This New England "Crucible" bit always gives Martin a kick, though, truth-be-told, the filmmaker who asked for it put us both on edge as he shouted out stage directions and paced the room, purple erection in hand, no doubt dreaming of some underage Betty in a community theatre league.

"Murderer!" that filmmaker yelled, claiming he wanted to ignite a greater "sense of tragedy" in me.

"Murderer!" Martin laughs out the line, remembering.

Allan breathes harder. He kneels to the ground. He closes his eyes.

"Only sport at the beginning," I say again.

"Time's up," Martin cuts in.

"Only a game," I say, offering my fetishized Salem. Lonely girls. Lost ships. Tiresome sea.

"Time." Martin says it again.

Afterward, Martin and I walk through the dim corridor. He lets out a whistle once we're in the elevator, counting the bills in his hands. "You get a load of this tip?"

When we pass the fountain in the lobby, I tell Martin to stop. "I need another wish," I say.

He opens his wallet and hands me a dime.

"Don't you want to know what I'm wishing?" I ask, but he's already heading toward the front door.

In the fountain, the fish circle their cheap pilgrim ship. Sheltered safely inside their bluer than blue, they don't even twitch when I throw in my dime. I watch it sink to the bottom without sound.

Martin blares the car horn outside the front door.

"What we need is a good meal," I say as I buckle myself in next to him. "Something real in our stomachs."

We find a steak house and hustle in, ordering two plates of prime rib. I laugh with the waitress, making conversational jokes to feel sane, but as soon as she leaves, I can feel something's not right again.

"Martin?"

He inspects his beer like it's something interesting.

Years from now, we'll be lying in other people's arms. We'll look back and laugh out loud, remembering these times, trying to imagine what had ever been "us."

What people won't do, we'll say to our friends, trying to talk it out of our systems.

It will be me who betrayed us. I put heart and soul into what we wanted. I even had a little fun. I thought this was *our* game.

I grab Martin's wrist across the table.

"You think less of me than you used to," I begin.

"Stop, Ruthie," Martin says.

A Slight Change in Tuesdays

I DON'T KNOW HOW the tradition started, but that whole year Fred and I never cooked dinner on Tuesdays. Word must have gone around that we treated our bachelors well because there was never any difficulty securing one. One year, fifty-two Tuesdays, fifty-two men we convinced to cook dinner for us.

When it was Fred's Tuesday to come up with a guy, he usually scouted out soured divorcés, those born-again bachelors found near squash courts and running tracks. I preferred new faces at the bar next to the lingerie shop I manage on the south side of our prissy New England town.

Dart throwers made the best cooks. They knew how to concentrate. Regardless of our hunting grounds, each chef had his own "specialty."

Fred and I often laughed over the "specialty" phenomenon after the bachelor of the week was on his way home with a smile on his face and a little bag of leftovers in hand. It is, of course, common lore that most men know how to cook two or perhaps three different dishes, so they pick one and call it their "specialty." A specialty sounds better than admitting they can't make anything else.

"You're just jealous," Fred always said if I tsked-tsked our men on this matter, "because you can't cook anything." He'd launch into his spiel about how he had not one but two specialties—shepherd's pie and "Jagannath Puri channe dal," a recipe he claimed he'd memorized from a Hari Krishna cookbook. He also liked to say that because he had two dishes and I didn't have any—he was twice the cook I was.

Fred likes to believe numbers can prove anything.

Anyway, guys and their specialties. Charles from Chattanooga—chicken chat with chutney. Sol from San Diego—"the Red Odyssey," a seven-course adventure comprised entirely of red foods. Lichen, giggly and waiflike, tried to tease us with "spore fruit." "A pear, if you will," he whispered, lifting an invisible object from an imaginary bowl, fingers fluttering as he wiped "spore" juice from his chin. Roch, an optometry student from Quebec, served up a savory tuber stew. "Nothing in there that doesn't grow underground," he said, giving the long silver ladle a flick.

Some of our bachelors got a little showy.

I believe it was Fred who went out and bought the white chef's hat and corresponding full-length apron. We never required our Tuesday night chefs to wear them. We simply hung the hat and the apron from an obvious peg in the kitchen. After all the fawning and cooing we made over each one, it amused us to see how quickly those whites went on.

As he cooked, we'd fix his favorite drink, and several of ours, and let our bachelor serve us his specialty. Everyone had a great dinner—everyone had a great time—that was the single requirement, and until Drexler, Tuesdays went off without a hitch.

Drexler distinguished himself immediately when he rang the bell at five o'clock, hours earlier than any of our other Tuesday night chefs. I was recuperating from a wretched day at the shop. An incompetent glass professional—"glazier," he insisted on my saying—had botched a perfectly straightforward job of dressing room mirror tilting.

I opened the door, still trying to decide whether it would be less bothersome to send the overeager chef away for a couple of hours or let him in and ignore him.

Before I could speak, Drexler thrust two brown paper bags inside the door. "One more thing!" he called over his shoulder as he rushed toward a Volkswagen bug parked near the curb.

As I waited, I scanned our prim cul-de-sac. No one watching our premises, for once.

Drexler returned with an elaborately decorated soup tureen. "I'm Drexler," he said. "And this is my tureen."

"Ruthie," I said.

"And them?" Drexler nodded toward the enameled figures on the tureen.

"Hello?" I said, uncertain whether I was to welcome them along with him.

"Kitchen?" He stepped inside, forcing me to back away as I continued to stare at the tureen. It was a clichéd scene, people playing guitars and flutes while children danced on the grass. There were animals, little goats and sheep, and a man clasping a long-haired woman who reached for the lacquered green outskirts of a forest.

Pleased with my reaction, Drexler tucked the tureen under his arm and, as if by instinct, turned kitchen-wise, grabbing one paper bag on his way.

"Excuse me," I said, picking up the other bag as I followed him. "How do you know Fred?"

Drexler didn't answer.

In the kitchen, Drexler lined up vials of spices and bundles of fresh herbs in a fussy order on the counter. With great ceremony, he pulled out a dark brown bottle with a French label. "Vanilla," he mouthed, running his finger across the red lettering. Then he began a brief inventory of our setup, opening drawers and cupboards, shaking his head.

"Am I glad I came prepared," he said with a sniff as he yanked a jar of expired rosemary from a shelf, throwing it into the trash can.

I was used to casual arrogance from our other Tuesday night chefs. Drexler's disgust offended me. "Make yourself at home," I said in a tone I hoped sounded brittle.

Drexler held up our chef's hat with two fingers, inspecting it with obvious distaste before he stuffed it into a drawer and pulled out his own. He posed in profile. Vertical starched pleats sat stiffly on top of his head.

"Adds a little stature, don't you agree?"

I dumbly nodded.

He tied our full-length apron around his neck and waist. "Sloppy, sloppy," he remarked, smoothing the wrinkled cotton with both hands. "And a bit conservative for my taste, Ruthie," he added. "If you want the truth."

"All I want is a drink," I said.

"I'll be having Tanqueray, then," Drexler said. "With just a spit of tonic. That's part of the deal, isn't it? I do dinner, you two do the drinks?"

"Sure," I said. "Part of the deal."

I walked into the next room and down our stone staircase to our defunct wood-burning stove that serves as our liquor cabinet. I cut up a lime and poured two stiff drinks, desperately trying to will Fred home in my mind.

In any story of our lives, the house must be described, although until one sees it, our home is never one to be believed. Built into a natural hill, it's a split-level affair designed for solar heating by our high-principled predecessors—one of Fred's architect colleagues—who, with his wife, had invested in a holistic pyramid scheme (powdered blue-green algae), bringing in the means to abandon this "dream home" and our teary New England for a sunnier coast.

The wing housing our bedrooms and bathrooms is tastefully spare. It's the "living" area that sets our quarters apart. A natural stone ledge, level with the kitchen and the rest of the house, serves as an open dining loft perched dramatically over a steep drop from which our living room can be viewed below. In the center of that ledge, a freestanding doorframe—The Portal! those former dreamers explained to us— marks the top of a staircase cut into the stone that descends via one sharp switchback to the moss-colored tile floor.

Notable amenities acquired with the house include the wood-burning stove, cold in our custody, a pullout fire-walking platform, two cascading fountains that trickle down the ledge, and, displayed high on the wall, an enormous peacock fan that once graced the head of a Las Vegas showgirl, a former love partner of both previous inhabitants. Her sudden death, they explained, marked the end of the "third level" of their spiritual evolution. For this reason, the feathers had to be "shed" to facilitate their progression into the fourth.

I can't exactly recall the crack Fred made in response to this tale— something about sticking the new owners with their woo-woo trash. All I remember is that it nearly cost us our home.

The room's masterpiece, however, is the floor-to-ceiling window that overlooks the Meadows, the nature preserve that surrounds our cul-de-sac, offering in daytime a view of our ever-changing New England swamps and grasses. But at night, the dark window reflects the Portal, the stone ledge, and the mossy flooring, creating a valley-like effect.

"We've hit the Bottoms, babe," Fred laughed the first night we found ourselves alone on the couch, dwarfed by the architectural effect.

To my chagrin, ever since, "The Bottoms" it's been.

By the time Fred arrived that evening, I'd changed into a silk kimono and silk pants and was sitting on the couch in the "living" area, thumbing through the daily edition of a competitor's mail-order lingerie catalog. A second iced drink tinkled in my hand.

"Smells great," Fred said as he rounded our switchback. I'd turned on the fountains higher than usual to mute the sounds of Drexler's enthusiasm in the kitchen above us.

Fred kissed my cheek when he reached me. "Who is it?"

"Very funny," I said.

Upstairs, Drexler broke into an accomplished tenor once again.

"Goat Song," I explained. "His favorite musical."

Fred sat on the couch, laughing.

"Fred, stop it. I mean it. Where did you find this one?"

Drexler appeared above us. He stood in the Portal, grinning beneath his ridiculous hat. "Hello, Fred," he called down. "I thought I heard you come in. I can't seem to find the fresh cilantro."

If there is fresh cilantro in shepherd's pie or Jagannath Puri channe dal, Fred drew a blank.

"Cilantro," Drexler said again, exaggerating the pronunciation. He took a step down. "It's a basic ingredient. That's why I didn't bring any. I figured, what decent household doesn't keep fresh cilantro?"

Drexler had taken off his shirt in the kitchen. Long-limbed, a bit on the tallish side, dark hair cropped close to the skull, he wore that tasteful though tired little shave popular among our men that winter, a vertical strip of hair farmed just below the lower lip. He was attractive enough. You wouldn't blame either of us for inviting him.

"Just let it go," Fred was saying to Drexler. His voice hit that nasal tone that on occasion means trouble. "What difference will a few leaves make?"

Drexler pursed his lips and turned back for the kitchen.

"Is this guy for real or what?" Fred said when he'd gone.

I walked over to the stove to fix two drinks. I admit I enjoyed watching Drexler get under his skin.

Fred stared at his reflection in the window, loosened his tie, and ran his hand through his hair. "I've had some kind of a day," he said, which usually signals complications on a high-profile project, some dramatic something or other soon to interrupt the center of our New England town.

"It's nothing, hon," I said, handing him a glass, but he kept staring at his reflection.

In truth, Fred and I have always found the window a bit unnerving—that life-sized reminder of our humdrum life unfolding in our not-so-humdrum home. I even find the thick glass dangerous. I swear a magnified sunray will ignite this abandoned husk of a dream house one day, scorch a wobbly message down our wooden coffee table like those art projects made at summer camp.

"What would the sun write if you gave it a pen?" a playful and dreamy young bachelor once mused after I confided this fear.

We expelled that bachelor immediately.

Back on the higher level, Fred and I covered the dining table with our gold tablecloth. Fred picked at a wax stain with his thumbnail while I went to find my favorite candleholder, a papier-mâché angel made by my grandmother from repurposed church bulletins and issues of the *Mennonite Weekly Review*. Most of the angel's detail had worn off, leaving only a pinkish mouth and, on the skirt, leftover words from a prayer request for Bibles in the Congo.

"She's got no eyes," Fred said irritably. He never liked the thing.

"They wore off," I reminded him. Remembering the angel's better days, sans tapers, on the top of my family's Christmas tree, I raised her to the light and blew dust from her face, wondering if I had chosen to keep her through the years—or had she chosen to keep me?

"She never had eyes," Fred said.

"That's only since you've known her," I replied, feeling us on the verge of one of our senseless fights about nothings that could turn into somethings.

In the kitchen, Drexler started up "I Want to Be Happy" from *No, No, Nanette*.

"We'll need plates," I said to Fred, giving up the issue of angels and eyes, which we both knew wasn't one.

Fred laid down the plates while I surveyed the table. Though we'd gone to thrift stores and mixed and matched plates to create our own eclectic dish set, I had to admit that the blue and red tapers in the angel holder and the mishmash array of plates made a statement more tasteless than our intended kitsch.

But what did it matter, I rationalized that night and still consider now, what Drexler thought of us?

We're homeowners. We keep up our lawn. We support local artists, local farms, and fruit orchards. We recycle. Each fall, we purchase twenty small crocks filled with spreadable cheese to help the local high school marching band stomp its way to oblivion in knee-high white boots, dancing flag corps included. Dutifully, we camouflage ourselves each day as inspired young professionals pursuing young dreams and, despite the window situation, manage to conceal enough of our personal lives to be passed over as respectable folk living among others in our snug cul-de-sac.

For some reason, the figurines on Drexler's tureen remained in my mind. Too much gin on an empty stomach, perhaps, but their presence seemed more than that.

"Appetizers in three minutes," Drexler called out from our kitchen.

It was pathetic, my obsessing about what Drexler or any bachelor thought of us.

"Fred?" I asked as I laid the last piece of silverware. "Where did you meet Drexler?"

"Very funny, Ruthie," he said.

Drexler appeared holding a platter. This time I was certain Fred noticed Drexler's bare back because he had removed his pants as well, leaving only his underwear.

"The appetizers," Drexler said, pulling out a chair. "I hope you don't mind—" He paused. "But I don't have actual names for any of my dishes. I'm always worried a label will lock me into a recipe, and then what do you think would happen to my creativity, Fred?" Drexler leaned back and opened his legs wide. "Out the window."

"Wouldn't want to put a crimp in those creative powers, Drexler," Fred said loudly and stood. "Get you a drink?"

"Nothing for me," Drexler said. "Ruthie fixed one earlier." He speared a strange fritter shaped like a blowfish sitting on a bed of fresh parsley. "I don't like to drink too much. Dulls the senses." Lifting the fork to his mouth, he added, "I don't like to forget anything."

I went numb. Dreams, disappointments, responsibilities—people we knew wanted to forget everything.

"Righto," Fred said, abandoning me with Drexler.

"Please, Ruthie," Drexler said, pushing the platter toward me. "Try one."

Just another bachelor, I reassured myself. Just another Tuesday.

Drexler watched with anticipation as I picked up my knife and fork. I sliced through the crisp skin. I drew the moment out, wanting Fred to come back. A witness seemed important.

"What is it, exactly?"

"You tell me."

I bit down. A spice I'd never tasted before burned my tongue. I grabbed my water glass.

"Okay there, hon?" Fred asked, without a flicker of compassion as he emerged from the Bottoms, fresh drinks in each hand.

"Tell me, Ruthie," Drexler pleaded. "What do you think? Be honest."

My eyes watered. "I don't know what to say."

Satisfied, he picked up my plate and his. "Fred, you won't even try one?"

I sniffed from the spice. Fred stared at me without sympathy.

"Perhaps you need to work him up for the ride," I suggested to Drexler. Impulsively, I shared the story of a recipe from the *More-with-Less Cookbook* our father came back to again and again. "Our Children Love Liver." The meat disguised, cut into sticks, and dipped like french fries into ketchup.

Drexler stared at me in disbelief. "Deceit is not part of my repertoire," he said sharply, and turned for the kitchen. "Next course, soup!"

Fred handed me a paper napkin stamped with two grinning bunnies leftover from a recent bachelor's Easter extravaganza. "The joke is over, Ruthie. Just tell him to quit . . . now. Please."

"Fred," I whispered. "I don't know him. I really don't know him."

Fred shook his head.

"It must be a joke," I said. "You or I told some bachelor to come, and that bachelor sent someone else—"

Drexler returned, carrying the tureen. "Please bear in mind, the soup is not quite the same without fresh cilantro." He glared at Fred. "And in response to an earlier insult, I've composed a quick ditty."

He set the tureen on the table and stepped back to recite an impromptu poem titled "The Leaf's Complaint or The Difference a Few Leaves Make."

Fred and I watched dumbfounded as Drexler, naked beneath his apron, his bared collarbones shining with sweat, detailed the fate of a discouraged and undervalued bud who refuses to unfurl and organizes a strike throughout the entire leaf kingdom, resulting in the sun melting the brains of the formerly indifferent human folk.

"All in twelve lines," he boasted when finished. "An ode."

To avoid his gaze, I stared at the tureen. I saw flames creeping toward the figures despite their glazed postures of glee. Had the fire been there before? Of course it had. Hadn't it?

A ladle plunged into the tureen, startling me. Drexler tasted it, sighed, and then poured soup into a bowl.

"Ruthie?" he said. "Why don't you try? I trust *your* opinion. I can still make tweaks."

"Do what you want," I said. "I'll try it when you think it's ready."

Drexler looked hurt. "Fine," he said, picking up the tureen. The apron strings dangled against his bare skin as he turned for the kitchen.

"For God's sake, Ruthie!" Fred said. "Don't stare."

"He's naked," I said. "He's got nothing on."

"You really don't know him, do you?" Fred was whispering, more to himself than to me. "We don't know him."

"He looks familiar," I said. "That guy who works in the convenience store? Maybe we're just used to seeing him wearing that little orange cap."

"The convenience store? Ruthie! Who the hell is in our kitchen?"
I gripped my drink. I concentrated on concentrating.

"It was your week," Fred continued. "Wasn't it? It was your week to find someone. I'm certain."

"We should keep a little log," I offered hazily.

Fred nodded. "If we just knew whose week it was," he said, "then you or I could remember who—"

"We should keep track of these things. A log," I said again, although I was doubtful it would solve our current dilemma. In truth, we'd made mistakes in the past with disastrous results, Dueling Bachelors in the kitchen making caustic jokes among the cutlery.

"Goat Song" started up in the kitchen again.

"Fred?" I asked. "Is something burning?"

"If I find out this Drexler business is one of your jokes," Fred went on.

"Something is burning," I said, and stood.

"Ruthie!" Fred grabbed my arm. He blocked my way. "He was down to our apron and that damn hat—who knows which one he's wearing now? I'm not going in there, Ruthie," he said. "And you definitely aren't, either."

On the angel, the candles were melting wax down her sides. I couldn't remember which one of us had lit them or how long they'd been burning.

"We have to do something," I said. "One of us has to."

"Logic," Fred said. "We've got to think this situation out. Logically."

"There's a naked man we don't know," I began.

Fred nodded with encouragement.

"Making dinner for us . . . in our kitchen."

A crash sounded in the kitchen. "Oopsy-daisy!" we heard.

"And," I continued, "something may or may not be burning."

"Exactly," Fred said. "I have it!"

He dropped my wrist and turned for the Portal. In the window, I watched his reflection go down to the Bottoms and pull out two glasses the size of pitchers. He cracked out the ice along with the tonic and gin.

"To us," Fred said when he returned to the table.

"To Tuesdays," I said.

Glasses in hand, we saluted our flickering reflection in the window and tipped our heads back. By the time Drexler returned with the soup, Fred and I were our warm and welcome Tuesday night selves again, welcoming strangers. We treated Drexler like any of our Tuesday night bachelors who happened to be serving us in the buff.

"Mighty hot in that kitchen, Drex?" I remember Fred saying.

"Are we all having a good time?" Drexler replied in a singsong voice. "That is my only requirement."

On the tureen, the flames had taken over. The people were gone but had left behind their instruments, a guitar and tambourine, a red cape, and a hoop-shaped plaything.

We laughed a lot from that course onward. Drinks flowing, I conducted rounds of cheers, saludos, and şerefes. Fred took off his shirt to make Drexler feel more at home. We attempted to teach Drexler a medley of songs from *West Side Story*, which he kept turning into "How Do You Solve a Problem Like Maria?" Mixed into the mood was a trio of Cornish hens stuffed with green olives and almonds and a proper English trifle served with a tray of brightly colored marzipan representing a past season Nativity scene he'd bought on a whim as it was discounted after the holiday.

Drexler kept making jokes about the edible baby and what he called the opposite end of "that whole Nativity cycle"—our endless rounds of Last Tuesday Night Suppers.

"Who will it be?" he asked, looking at Fred and then at me. "Who will betray whom?"

Fred ate the Wise Men. I ate the star. Drexler polished off six bite-sized shepherds as streams of red and blue wax ran down the angel's unseeing eyes.

After dinner, we made our way down to the Bottoms and explained to Drexler our tradition of Tuesday Night Charades. Those guessing were only allowed to watch the actor's reflection in the glass. But Drexler would only perform Dead Baby Jokes, which was fine enough in the first round. He rolled somersaults around the room and landed in a fetal position, naked as he was, on our cold tile floor.

"Dead Baby in the Dryer!" Fred finally called out, laughing as Drexler nodded.

Drexler stumped us in the second round by spinning madly and landing, limbs akimbo with his tongue hanging out. He spun again and landed in an equally contorted position. "Dead Baby in a Kaleidoscope," Drexler said curtly after we gave up.

"Bravo!" Fred clapped enthusiastically.

Losers.

I swear I heard Drexler say the word under his breath as he stood soberly in front of us.

Fred and I took our turns again.

"No more Dead Baby Jokes," I insisted as Drexler prepared for his final round. He had requested a full-length mirror, which Fred had hauled down from our bedroom. Drexler propped the mirror against the stove, facing the window.

"Dead Baby Jokes are jokes," I explained. "Not charades. There's a difference. Fred... isn't there a difference? Tell him, jokes aren't charades."

"Charades are charades, Ruthie," Fred said irritably. "Don't get complicated."

"Thank you, Fred," Drexler said. "My feelings exactly."

Drexler lay on his back with his head close to the window. He arched his upper spine, lifted his chest, and pointed his chin toward the ceiling. His reflection in the window was reflected in the mirror, which reflected again his image in the window—the replication continued. The longer I stared, the more his spine opened grotesquely into the pose.

"Guess," Drexler rasped impatiently, the posture constricting his throat.

"Dead Baby in a Petri Dish?" I tried, going along with the game only because I wanted him to stop.

"Not bad," Fred complimented me.

Drexler didn't move.

"Dead Baby... beneath a microscope?"

"Cold," Drexler gasped.

I slammed down my glass. The mirror rattled against the stove. "Stop it," I said. "That's not charades. That's not how the game goes!"

"Dead Baby in a Mad House?" Fred tried, staring at all of us reflected in the window.

"Warm," Drexler sighed. "But you people will never get it until you watch from outside."

"Right!" Fred said. Giddy and in the spirit of things, he reached for my hand.

I resisted.

"Ruthie?" Drexler said. "This is not the time to question everyone else's fun."

Fred pulled me up the stairs. As we crossed beneath the Portal, I looked back. In the window, our reflection shimmered, pale and ghostly, at the top of the ledge.

Drexler saw my hesitation. "Go," he demanded. "I've just given you a clue."

"This is a mistake," I said to Fred, but he was too lost in the game.

"Come on, Ruthie!" He pulled me toward the front door.

The lock clicked behind us. I heard it as we rushed onto the front step and faced our cul-de-sac, our dead end glowing with suburban calm.

"This is a mistake," I said again.

But Fred had already passed the garage and turned for the hill that slopes down to our backyard. "I have it," Fred called out. "Dead Baby . . . dead baby . . . I think I know!"

I followed, running to keep up.

As we stood in our backyard, the living room shone before us. In the mirror, our shadowy forms hovered like two intruders staring into their own home. The peacock fan trembled against the wall, sensitive as always to invisible air currents. Our catalogs and magazines, a red silk robe I'd cast off days ago, empty glasses and shakers—all appeared dwarfed and ridiculous beneath the expansive proportions of the room.

Drexler's contortion had deepened even more. His rib cage lifted and widened, revealing the softness below the solar plexus as it rose and fell with his breath.

Fred cupped his hands on the window. "Dead Baby in a Fun House!" he shouted through the glass.

"Stop," I said to Drexler. "Stop!" I said to Fred.

"Dead Baby in a Fun House," Fred shouted again.

The answer must have been correct because Drexler stood up. He slipped his arms inside my silk robe and raised the glass I'd left on the stove. He threw himself onto the couch with a drunken, matronly scowl on his face and made a familiar flick with his wrist.

"That's you!" Fred laughed.

"Side-splitting," I said.

"Genius," Fred insisted.

Discarding the robe, Drexler started laughing and slapping his knee, as Fred often does. But Fred was too far gone to get angry.

"Fred," I said. "Fred?"

But he only had that pleased look that means he's had too much to drink, even for him. He dropped to the grass in a happy stupor.

Behind us, Drexler sat down as Fred did, nodding and grinning.

"Stop!" I shouted, slamming my hands on the glass.

I heard Fred go down, and then Drexler too fell back, belly up.

He'd gotten the best of me. Furiously, I ran to the front of the house and rang the bell. I slammed my palm on the door. "Locked out," I shouted.

Drexler ignored me.

I turned away from the door and stared at the sleepy circle of dark windows and porch lights. "Locked out," I said to no one.

Slowly, I returned to the backyard. Inside the house, our lights still shone. Drexler remained on the floor. I turned and slid down the window, sitting in the grass.

"Fred!" I said, giving his shoulder a shake, though it was clear he wouldn't move on his own for some time. I pulled his head onto my lap, covering him with the sleeves of my kimono. Drexler moved and pressed his back against mine on the other side of the window, our naked, creature-like warmth transferring through the glass.

As I anchored our strange assembly, the clear night struck me with calm. Surrounded by the Meadows, the ever-evergreens, and the distant stars, our lights seemed whimsical—our lives inside these busy circles nothing more than a dream.

Finally, sleep came for me too, bringing a serenade of the abandoned guitars and tambourines I'd seen on the tureen along with memories of fire.

The sun woke us, blazing indifferently on the window as it did every morning. I covered my eyes until I came to some semblance of aware-ness, and when I opened them, I saw a man pushing a baby jogger down the bike path. As they passed in front of us, the father nodded, as if he found Fred and I there, sleeping so, every morning.

The child grabbed the sides of its little chariot and looked out at the Meadows.

Can you hear them? I wanted to shout at the child, who for a moment wasn't that child, but the child I once had been. Can you hear those sirens in the grasses, telling you something is lost? But then the previous night's haze and the morning sun morphed that ache of lost innocence into that race from ruin I'd seen on Drexler's tureen.

I turned to the window. In the sun's glare I saw only our own reflec-tion. I pressed my hands on the glass. Drexler was gone.

"Fred? Fred!"

Fred stirred in my lap.

"Wake up, Fred!"

He raised his hand to his eyes. "No more Tuesdays," he whispered. Our Tuesday Night Chef idea had had its day, he said, but that day too was gone.

Groggily, Fred and I made our way into the garage to search for the spare key that inserted us back into our everyday lives. A quick call to my lingerie shop assured me my girls were duly adorning our dreamers in the ordinary, pretty passions we supplied. Fred's secretary filled him in discreetly as she often did on Wednesdays, no longer expecting him to come in.

Drexler left no mark. His utensils, the herbs, his clothing, the tureen, even the leftovers—all were gone.

The only evidence of things gone awry was my papier-mâché angel sitting on the table in ruins. Her candles had burned too low, blackening her pulpy spirit for good. But the worst of it was that at some point during the previous evening, Drexler or Fred or perhaps even I had made tiny pinpricks where her eyes should have been, cut through to her hollow core.

I picked her up. I felt her lightness. Instead of throwing her into the trash, I put her into the sink and ran the hot water. She bent and then buckled, generations of prayer requests sliding down her until she too was lost, nothing but mulch.

The next Tuesday we went out. We've made a tradition of it every Tuesday with a group of carefully selected friends. They all know that moment will come when Fred lifts his glass.

"Traditions," he'll say, as if Tuesdays had always been this way and always would be.

"To Tuesdays," we cheer, heads nodding, marking time.

Faith Is Just Another Sorrow
Santos

JONAH'S GRANDCHILDREN, their five blond heads bleached white by sun, braced themselves before the next ocean wave. Their screams blended with those of the Brazilian children as the next crest peaked and broke, crushing them under its force. Anxiously, Jonah counted their emerging heads. Cyrus, and then Isabel. Eli. Finally the twins, Rachel and poor Ruthie, the youngest by only three minutes, her arms forever flailing.

Ruthie, identical to Rachel but somehow so fragile, so easily wrecked by opinions of others, would she make it? The most sensitive souls fledged in their family tree had their ways of coming quietly undone, one or two at least in each generation.

Jonah stood apart from the other adults, his cane anchored in the iridescent palm of an upturned shell. He tried not to lean too heavily on his good leg as his doctor advised the day before he and Mother boarded the plane in Canton-Akron for São Paulo, where their oldest daughter and her husband had served for the past ten years. Their younger daughter's family, including the twins, had flown in from a mission assignment in Paraguay to join them during the Christmas vacation.

Both daughters shared an old quilt spread on the sand with three Brazilian converts, two females and one male, who'd traded their saints for apostles the previous Sunday. Jonah and Mother had sat through the ceremony on an uncomfortable wooden bench as their oldest sped through the liturgy toward the ritual dousing—no showy dunking, thank God!—while a skinny fellow with a guitar wrecked perfectly good hymns with bossa nova interpretations.

The converts wept openly during the service, consumed by emotions that seemed genuine but made the entire affair wholly unlike—not wrong, simply unlike—the efficient and modest baptismal sprinklings witnessed in congregations of their particular American Mennonite conference.

Still, this was one of Jonah's proudest successes. That his daughters, missionaries stationed in Brazil and Paraguay, had served and would continue to serve even after he and Mother were both gone.

Jonah stabbed the seashell with the butt of his cane. These were the thoughts of a dying man!

"Dad!" Joy stood on the quilt. "We didn't see you there."

Jonah looked away. The "swimsuit" Joy wore was actually a dress. It contrasted too markedly with the string numbers worn by real Brazilians, even the converts who sat near her. He didn't approve. Such modesty had vanity in it. In this country, even he bared his puny leg to the world.

"Really, Dad. You're all alone back there!"

Jonah could feel Joy was going to ask *what are you thinking?* His daughters' endless attempts to rummage through his words for memories or, even worse, profound truths, these made him feel old.

"Leave me *be*," he said as good-naturedly as he could.

At the water's edge Cyrus yelled and held up a shell. The children gathered around him. After a brief inspection, Eli and Isabel turned away, no longer interested. Cyrus threw the shell back onto the sand, where Ruthie stared at it desperately. She squeezed her small fists, certain she missed something everyone else could see.

Poor Ruthie. She didn't get there was nothing to get.

The other children, even Rachel, laughed at Ruthie's frustration, knowing their laughter would crush her.

Jonah felt tired. Though he liked the family best out there, near the water, where he could see their bodies and hear their laughter, but also where they didn't feel obliged to include him in conversation or annoy him with mindless chatter, he turned to make his way toward the cottage, where Mother worked steadily in the kitchen. She was in her glory—or so everyone assumed—cooking for three generations and the converts who'd caravanned with them to their oldest daughter's summer cottage in Santos, eighty kilometers south of São Paulo. At the cottage door, Jonah glanced back. Children strung themselves along the water's edge all the way down the beach. Others wandered into the waves. He envied them, so innocent of currents, unaware of the water's dark force. Some were drawn farther out, dangerously far, believing themselves invincible as children do.

On the third day of their vacation, thunder rolled over the ocean. Dark clouds covered the sun by ten in the morning, turning the olive-green water to brackish blue.

"Cumulonimbus clouds," Cyrus informed Jonah with the tone of an impatient schoolmaster. "Or a cyclone."

"We should leave," Jonah said, first to the boy and then to everyone inside the cottage.

But his daughters—so nostalgic for his wisdom they trailed him at times with a goddamn tape recorder—refused to listen when his words inconvenienced their vacation plans.

They'd waited out other storms, Joy insisted. They knew the tropics.

A swift glance from Mother confirmed she agreed with *him*, but she only went into the kitchen and began cooking again, this time in preparation for an emergency.

The ocean's agitation intensified throughout the morning. In the surrounding cottages, men began securing roofs, nailing windows shut, and covering doors with tarps. Jonah picked up a hammer and joined the efforts of his sons-in-law, one whistling incessantly "Blowin' in the Wind" as if their task were a joke. They drove nails into plywood planks, covering the cottage windows.

The urgency of the task made Jonah feel alive. Sweat broke across his brow. As the grandchildren carried out drinks and sandwiches from the kitchen, they admiringly looked up at him.

After the cottage had been secured, the converts wisely packed up and hitched a ride with the other Brazilians abandoning the shore. By late afternoon, only their family remained on the beach, six adults and five children, the *americanos* braced before the ocean storm.

At first, the children delighted in their isolation. "A deserted island!" they shouted as their parents sealed them inside the cottage, cocooning them even tighter inside their illusion of—Jonah couldn't imagine what.

Confined, Jonah sat in the living room with his sons-in-law, who discussed predictable topics. Desperation in the *favelas*. Drug lords and dictators. Alfredo Stroessner, in the game still. Elvis, dead on the crapper. Missionary boards always putting First World pressures on them—numbers! budgets!—as they sweated and prayed and gave their very lives to matters of sickness and education, to the welfare of souls.

Jonah stared at his palms, still raw from gripping the hammer. He'd never been adept at articulating his thoughts. Self-conscious of his rural education, he either had no opinion at all or feelings so strong his words erupted in outbursts his seminarian sons-in-law disliked. Even Mother said his emotions discredited him. And the storm had already put him out of sorts. Swings in barometric pressure always played havoc with his nerves.

The children galloped into the room and threw their bodies onto the floor, squealing with the same tension.

Jonah focused on the row of papier-mâché angels Mother had made with the children the previous week, days before Christmas, repurposing church bulletins and past issues of the *Mennonite Weekly Review*. The angels sat in a row on top of a tea cart. The least well-made was beginning to buckle, head and halo drooping with a hollow sadness, likely a reaction to the moist air.

Wind rattled the front door. The other men continued their talk. Were they only pretending not to notice?

Unable to endure the noise any longer, Jonah went into the kitchen. Mother sat at the table, her shoulders squared against their daughters' simultaneous attempts to trump the other's goodwill efforts, a senseless competition they'd carried out since their teenage years.

This pained Jonah. To continue this way as the very walls shook—

"All of it is meaningless, a chasing after the wind," he said.

Startled, they turned.

"Ecclesiastes," he said.

"Qoheleth!" One of the seminarians had the audacity to "correct" Jonah from the other room. His daughters, his wife, the men—everyone laughed at him.

Jonah pretended to laugh with them, hiding the tears that so maddeningly burned in his eyes as he made his way to the only private room in the tiny cottage, graciously assigned to Mother and him. He heaved himself onto the mattress that reeked of mold and the American mothballs his daughter hauled back by the bushel.

The wind roared again. Waves crashed onto the receding shoreline, moving closer to them. The storm would be a bad one. Jonah felt a dark satisfaction. He'd been right! Everything changes. Nothing does. Ecclesiastes or Qoheleth.

Jonah fell asleep.

Jonah woke to a commotion. Ruthie was receiving a round of fearful reprimands for trying to break through the front door long after being told there was no leaving, perhaps for days. Ruthie, of course, sensitive as Jonah was to barometric swings, that cold nervousness that intensified in the body's cavities, those strange fingers that tightened around an already anxious heart.

Searching for escape, Ruthie threw open his bedroom door. "Grandfather?"

"Yes, child?"

Poor Ruthie. She was still too young to recognize that others didn't feel the same sensations or the storm's approach as they both did.

If they made it through this—there, Jonah allowed himself the complete thought—if they all made it through *this*, the body-fearing manners of their faith would still terrorize this child. How long would she mistake her fierce pulls of emotion for unpardonable sins? The family never spoke of Jonah's youngest brother, who had administered a shot to his own head long before his daughters were born.

But here was Ruthie, so eerily like him, a physical child demanding physical truths, one more who might mistake her difference for deficiency.

"Grandpa?" Ruthie's voice grew anxious as she peered into his dark room.

"Still here, child," Jonah reassured her. Yes, this child too was theirs only for the upbringing. She would leave them one day or go mad. "Still here."

Ruthie shut the door. Jonah turned toward the wall, wondering at the distinct pain in his gut that survived so many years. *Still here, child.*

He missed his brother.

Later, after the family plowed through more prayers, Mother's rice and beans, and the remains of the previous day's passionfruit cobbler, the children performed the same reenactments they'd staged on Christmas Day in São Paulo, stock duets the adults had no choice but to watch.

Abraham trembling before Isaac on the old chopping block. Samson undone again by a cloying Delilah.

The girls' preoccupation with the story of Naomi, Ruth, and Boaz baffled Jonah. Was it faith, love, or some other sorrow that fixated them on the minor tale? They'd learn soon enough what held or did not hold those stories together, that the plots they so obediently performed were illusion and not the point anyway.

Finally, the full ensemble stumbled through a Nativity scene—Cyrus as Joseph stood passively beside Isabel, who swaddled an emptied Clorox bottle. Eli and Rachel doubled as shepherds and towel-turbaned kings as Ruthie dithered nervously between ass and angel.

The children's relationship to the text was so physical. Memorized monotone. Childish thrusts of prayer he could appreciate in better moods. But on that night in Santos as the storm intensified, their antics only echoed useless heartache.

"But Mary treasured up all these things and pondered them in her heart." Luke 2. Verse 19. How many years would pass until they felt these words as knives and, once felt, realized how these ponderings, the mysteries, did not stop?

"Dad? Dad! What are you thinking?" Attention veered directly to him.

"Leave me be," Jonah said darkly, unable to come up with another response. Another family moment ruined by him, though that wasn't what he wanted.

After the show, as his daughters put the children into sleeping bags in the living room with prayers and songs, his sons-in-law escaped to a storage closet with a short-wave radio. When the adults reconvened around the kitchen table, the men reported news in whispers.

There was no changing course. The roads had washed out. And the worst of the storm still approached.

Jonah stared at his hands. He'd been right.

He avoided Mother's eyes. How many years had she silently witnessed his successes and then buttressed his failures? Choices in crops and planting times, perennial gambles. Selling silos to augment losses. Their beloved barn, burned to the ground.

Here in Santos, he failed the family again. After years of reading the sky, he knew its overhead moods and shifts better than any of them. He should have demanded they leave. He should have started the car and threatened to drive off alone if they didn't listen.

Jonah looked up. His wife and daughters and even his sons-in-law had bowed their heads, assuming he was praying.

"Dear Lord, blessed are these children," he said wearily. The words would have to suffice.

"We're going to die!"

Ruthie stood in the doorway. Ruthie, of course. Too fragile. Already, this child felt too much. *She won't make it.*

"Dad!" Joy said.

If Jonah had said the last words aloud, he hadn't meant to.

"We're going to die!" Ruthie cried again.

No one answered her.

The generator shut down during the night. The children ate breakfast by candlelight as their mothers searched for the old kerosene lamp, found—*thanks to the Lord*—in a forgotten cabinet. The adults did their best to hide their concerns, but the children knew better and hovered fearfully around the table even after they finished eating.

Joy maintained her grip on Ruthie, still emanating her dreams of escape. Mother leaned against the counter beside their older daughter. His sons-in-law went into the front room to investigate the ceiling for a spot they might break through if the cottage flooded. If need be, they could all wait for help on the roof.

Help from whom, the seminarians didn't specify.

Like wafers offered at other peoples' last rites, family mythologies were doled out. Mother contributed her old ordeal. Her father had been chosen to serve as deacon in their home church, but the appointment was blocked. He hadn't been selected by lot—the Lord's voice had not been consulted. So, by lot, another man was chosen. Shamed by the Lord in front of the congregation, her father hadn't been allowed to lead.

Sixty years ago, Jonah wanted to shout. He had no idea why his wife harbored that old fury after their own daughters had faithfully founded churches of their own. But this was her family's hurt, her generation defined by its perception of that single disgrace. She would cling to the slight until her end.

A thundering wave crashed just beyond the front room.

Desperate to distract the children, his daughters veered into romanticized versions of how they met their husbands. The children perked up. They'd heard the stories before but knew that in these chance meetings, they finally appeared. His oldest daughter met her husband in a soda shop in their northern Indiana college town. He'd bought her a triple scoop sundae called the "Pig's Trough"—the tired detail added to make the children laugh, and then, nothing but "happily ever after."

Smiling in the shadowy lamplight, his daughter appeared to believe in her tale, though Jonah distinctly remembered she'd come to them at least twice pregnant and in tears just before Cyrus was born.

Joy told her story next. They met on a short-term relief mission in Haiti. "We knew immediately," she said, tousling Rachel's hair. No mention of her first fiancé, a poet Jonah liked, who suffered a quiet breakdown after nursing too lovingly the sad stirrings strained through their particular Mennonite gene pool.

As winds roared outside, Jonah felt a dull realization. These versions weren't lies. Chance meetings and successes, decisions and guesses, uncomfortable compromises—like the Bible itself, stories *required* revision both to serve and to survive.

The men returned from the front room, their faces tense. Bristling with forced cheer, Joy tried to get the children to sing "With Christ in Your Boat, You Can Smile at the Storm," but they stumbled over words they knew well.

"Dad?" Joy demanded. "Your turn."

"A love story," his oldest chided.

"Mother?" Jonah prompted.

"You do it," she responded. "I can't concentrate."

Despite the sealed-off windows, the smell of the ocean's brine had intensified in the room. The bewildered clock above the refrigerator pointed its fingers at a night-dark noon.

Jonah cleared his throat. He knew the family expected the standard retelling of their meeting. How he and Mother met at a church social held in the Walnut Creek hollow. A simple picnic studded with prayers. The Lord revealed their partnership immediately. But this had never been the entire truth.

"Miriam," Jonah said, the sound of his first love's name surprising even him.

Mother shifted her weight against the counter.

"Miriam?" Joy said.

His daughters had likely never even considered the name aside from the Moses tale. But there had been a Miriam. An Old Order girl. His Miriam. Her casting away of him was a love story their very existence depended on.

Jonah began, describing how awkward glimpses at markets and farm sales grew into shy conversations, eventually laced with depths and vulnerabilities. He proposed, but Jonah's family belonged to a Swiss Mennonite community in Sonnenberg and Miriam's family to the Old Order near Homerville. Jonah's proposal was refused. Shattered by the rejection, predictable as it was, Jonah bought a 1933 Indian Scout and motorcycled out of Wayne and Holmes County with little money and no destination in mind.

Jonah hesitated. In the lantern's flickering, tomblike light, not one of his daughters or sons-in-laws interfered. He saw Ruthie's gaze, fixed on him. Could his story somehow save her?

In the 1930s, highways were hardly highways. Weaving on and off Route 66, he rode through open range, over gravel lanes. Some nights, he unrolled a tattered blue quilt made from his mother's old dresses and slept in open fields. As days became weeks, washroom mirrors revealed a stranger's unshaven face, tightly drawn inside a growing hurt.

Though he hadn't known it was his destination, he drove all the way to the West Coast. On Route 1 just south of San Francisco, he stood on a cliff and stared at the waves surging against the base of the granite wall.

There at the table, surrounded by storm, Jonah remembered the feel of the ocean's pull, how deeply he imagined merging with that force.

"Humility," he said, knowing they wouldn't get it.

He wasn't talking about the humility that shackled them to their faith, not that old obligation. He meant that humility required to turn around and drive home, the humility required to graft present over past, like skin over skin. Humility as knowing, humility as survival.

But if he tried to explain this, he would cry again, and they'd all stop listening.

"I was the one who wasn't supposed to make it," he said, leaving out how he came home to find his brother dead.

This story the adults already knew, even if they didn't know why Jonah hadn't been there.

Mother stared at the lamp.

"But you did make it," Joy said tersely—for the children. "You did."

Ruthie's lip trembled as if a betrayal had taken place, and perhaps it had.

One of Jonah's sons-in-law broke the tension, "Always the one who got away."

"What happened to the bike?" the other said. "Indian Scout? Worth something now."

His daughters laughed, eager to change the subject.

Jonah nodded. "A beauty," he said. Dismissed again, he'd succumbed to his emotions, a narcissist. Jonah left the table for the bedroom and lay down in the dark.

The walls shook when the first of two violent waves struck the cottage. Jonah heard windows shatter in nearby bungalows and then the forceful rush of sand and water sliding back in the undertow. Deciphering the children's screams in the next room, Jonah understood water had oozed in between the walls and floor. The cottage was threatening to lose its claw hold on the sandy base.

"Dad?" Joy forced open the bedroom door. "Dad!"

"Leave me be," Jonah said, surprised when she backed away, obeying him.

He slept through the second surge, learning the details afterward through Mother's whispered scolding. She was disappointed, she said, that he'd gone off on his own—he'd abandoned them—just when they thought the end was coming.

"The End, Mother?" Jonah said mockingly, grabbing her hand.

But Jonah was with them later, after Ruthie succeeded in breaking through the front door. At least some animal sense enabled the child to wait until the storm receded before she raced into the grim stillness of its aftermath. After Ruthie was dragged in, stuttering and shivering, her father tended to her mother, who'd collapsed in the corner after carrying their child for a quarter of a mile over washed-up debris, refusing to put her down, even after slicing her own foot on a piece of ravaged metal.

As the other adults consoled the remaining children, Jonah found himself alone with Ruthie in the kitchen. Hair matted, eyes wild, Ruthie's body shook as she tried to decipher what she'd just seen, that ancient truth—how small we all stand, braced before the indifferent force of the ocean.

"We're alive," Ruthie kept saying.

How many times would she find herself there? Would she manage, each time, to walk away? Here was reason to remain as long as one could. To show this child what it means to simply hold on. To find one's own way. Belief . . . faith . . . where had it gone?

"Child," Jonah said.

"We're alive, Grandpa," Ruthie said. "Here we are."

ACKNOWLEDGMENTS

THANK YOU TO Margot Livesey, who selected this manuscript for the John Simmons Short Fiction Award and to the staff at the University of Iowa Press, including James McCoy, Lily Giddings, Susan Hill Newton, Meghan Anderson, Allison Means, and Mason Hamberlin, among others, and my insightful copyeditor, Carolyn Brown.

My gratitude goes to the magazines and editors who published earlier versions of some of these stories: *So to Speak*, *Electric Literature*, *Fence*, *Ninth Letter*, *Cosmonauts Avenue*, *Fiction International*, and *Witness Magazine*. The title story was developed for the Mennonite/s Writing Conference VIII: Narratives of Place and Displacement, held at the University of Winnipeg in 2017; I thank the writers and organizers who continue that conference series.

Thank you also to institutions that provided fellowships and support during the writing of these stories, including the National Endowment for the Arts, the New York Foundation for the Arts, the Research Foundation at the City University of New York, our union PSC-CUNY, and New York City College of Technology.

For me, writing is a communal activity. I wish to thank the writers and friends who've read these stories and shared their own work along the way, including past and present members of the Exiles Writers Group; Mickey Hawley and Viet Dinh; and writer and editor Wah-Ming Chang.

Lastly, I thank my mother (who still questions the dangling preposition in this book's title) and my sisters for their limitless patience and acceptance; Kathy Royer and Raylene Hinz-Penner, my earliest writing role models. And, of course, I'm grateful to Massimo, for his humor and wisdom and shared inquiry into what any of our lives might be good for.

THE IOWA SHORT FICTION AWARD AND THE
JOHN SIMMONS SHORT FICTION AWARD WINNERS,
1970–2025

Lee Abbott
Wet Places at Noon
Cara Blue Adams
You Never Get It Back
Donald Anderson
Fire Road
Dianne Benedict
Shiny Objects
A. J. Bermudez
Stories No One Hopes Are about Them
Marie-Helene Bertino
Safe as Houses
Will Boast
Power Ballads
David Borofka
Hints of His Mortality
Robert Boswell
Dancing in the Movies
Mark Brazaitis
The River of Lost Voices: Stories from Guatemala

Jack Cady
The Burning and Other Stories
Pat Carr
The Women in the Mirror
Kathryn Chetkovich
Friendly Fire
Cyrus Colter
The Beach Umbrella
Marian Crotty
What Counts as Love
Jennine Capó Crucet
How to Leave Hialeah
Jennifer S. Davis
Her Kind of Want
Janet Desaulniers
What You've Been Missing
Sharon Dilworth
The Long White
Susan M. Dodd
Old Wives' Tales
Thomas A. Dodson
No Use Pretending

Annabel Thomas
The Phototropic Woman
Jim Tomlinson
Things Kept, Things Left Behind
Douglas Trevor
*The Thin Tear in the Fabric
of Space*
Laura Valeri
The Kind of Things Saints Do
Anthony Varallo
This Day in History
Ruvanee Pietersz Vilhauer
*The Water Diviner and Other
Stories*
Sharon Wahl
*Everything Flirts:
Philosophical Romances*

Don Waters
Desert Gothic
Lex Williford
Macauley's Thumb
Miles Wilson
Line of Fall
Russell Working
Resurrectionists
Emily Wortman-Wunder
Not a Thing to Comfort You
Ashley Wurzbacher
Happy Like This
Charles Wyatt
Listening to Mozart
Don Zancanella
Western Electric